Allie reached over, took the journal from Brett's hands and laid it on the end table. Brett finally looked up. Allie wasn't wearing anything except a diamond and gold heart necklace Brett had given her years ago.

Brett gasped as Allie straddled her legs and sat on her lap, leaning down to brush Brett's lips with her own. Brett stroked the soft smoothness of Allie's thighs, then the plushness of her breasts. Her nipples were already hard little peaks gracing the nearly white skin. She leaned forward to grab a nipple in her mouth as Allie stretched and arched to offer it to her. She held it in her teeth as her tongue played across it, teasing it until it became even larger. She cupped both Allie's breasts in her hands and brought them together, her tongue swishing back and forth across them, then she took both nipples simultaneously in her mouth.

Allie cupped her own breasts so that Brett was free to explore her naked flesh. She ran her short fingernails down Allie's back, then reached down to cradle Allie's ass. She pulled the cheeks apart and ran a finger near the opening. Allie moaned in enjoyment, arching further still so that Brett had to catch her in her arms.

"Why don't we go upstairs?" Allie said breathily. Brett picked Allie up, carried her to their bedroom and threw Allie on the bed, then quickly undressed herself.

WHEN THE DEAD SPEAK

The Second Brett Higgins Mystery

THERESE SZYMANSKI

THE NAIAD PRESS, INC.
1998

Printed in the United States of America on acid-free paper
First Edition

Editor: Christine Cassidy
Cover designer: Bonnie Liss (Phoenix Graphics)
Typesetter: Sandi Stancil

Library of Congress Cataloging-in-Publication Data

Szymanski, Therese, 1968 –
  When the dead speak : a Brett Higgins mystery / Therese
Szymanski.
      p.   cm.
   ISBN 1-56280-198-8   (pbk.)
   I. Title.
PS3569.Z94W5   1998
813'.54—dc21   97-52959
                                                                  CIP

For Teri (1958–1995)
and
Gloria (1954–1978)

Although they are no longer with us,
they speak to us every day,
for they touched our lives
and will live on in our hearts, minds and souls,
and through their children.

About the Author

Therese Szymanski is an award-winning playwright who works in advertising and plays in theater — with both *POW* (*Pissed Off Wimmin*) and *Alternating Currents*. She enjoys hanging around in extremely unsavory neighborhoods, has never been accused of political correctness and finds most of her past too strange to share with anyone until at least the second date.

She lives in Royal Oak, Michigan, with the greatest little fagboy around and his dog, Astro, an eight-year-old Labrador who can't decide if he's a puppy or a person.

PROLOGUE
November 13, 1967

The cold, harsh winds of a Michigan November beat furiously against the two-story, white-sided house as Liza and Jen pressed into each other, naked and sweating. Heedless of the chill air seeping in through the windows, Liza threw the last of the blankets off as she fast approached orgasm. Sweat broke out all over her naked body while she writhed across her bed, being pushed further and further toward the edge of no return by her lover's caresses and touches.

A car door banged shut in the driveway, followed by the opening and closing of the front door. Jen looked up from between Liza's legs and Liza pulled herself off of Jen's fingers as the intruder pounded snowy boots on the front entry carpet.

"Shit!" Liza urgently whispered. "Someone's home!"

The two hurriedly dressed. Liza hoped it was only Elise, deciding to play hooky from school with her after all, because their mother's afternoon card group, across town, usually lasted until early evening, and their dad didn't arrive home from work until 5:30, sharp.

"You'd better get out of here," Liza told Jen, directing her to the window so she could climb down the trellis. Jen paused, reached over and kissed Liza on the lips.

"I love you," she said, before disappearing out the window to climb carefully down the icy trellis. She would run down the street to the store where she had left her car.

Liza went downstairs, figuring it was Elise, her twin sister. Of course, it might just be a neighbor come to borrow a cup of sugar, except all the neighbor women were playing cards across town with her mother. Regardless, Liza wasn't afraid. Crime didn't really exist in 1967 in Alma, Michigan. Even if an occasional hippie vagabond came to town looking for a hand-out as he journeyed across America, he was certain to leave once he realized nothing ever happened in Alma.

"Elise?" Liza called out.

* * * * *

2

A few hours south in Detroit, a doctor was finishing a surprisingly short and uncomplicated birth. He slapped the pink-faced baby across the butt and looked at the mother.

"Congratulations, Mrs. Higgins," he said, handing the baby to Alice. "It's a girl!"

Although the girl was Alice Higgins' first daughter after six boys, she wasn't happy. She never wanted a baby girl. Girls only grew up to carry their mothers' burdens all over again.

CHAPTER ONE

Brett's phone rang. There was a woman who wanted to audition as a dancer. She went down the long dark staircase and out to the small lobby.

The woman was gorgeous, with thick, wavy long dark hair, deep, intense eyes and olive-colored skin. Brett slowly looked her up and down before meeting her gaze. She guessed her to be sixteen, even though her body, which Brett could just barely see outlined through her loose-fitting, dirty clothes, looked more mature. Jailbait, illegal, child molestation/exploitation . . .

But the dark eyes drew her in.

"Take your clothes off," Brett said.

The woman looked stunned. "Here?" she asked. "But it's so . . ."

"Open? Public?" Brett teased, circling her like a jungle cat assessing its prey. "But that's what stripping is all about, hon," she said, running a hand down the woman's arm. Every moment was as if it happened yesterday, but also somehow surreal, imagined, bigger-than-life.

The woman turned to her and slowly began to unbutton her shirt, their gazes still locked. The shirt, the faded army jacket that already lay on the impossibly dirty floor, as well as the girl's worn jeans and shoes, spoke of someone in need. As if she still wore the clothes she had run away from home in.

The shirt dropped to the floor. She wore no bra. Her breasts were quite full for a girl her age — Brett could imagine cupping them in her hands, nibbling at the already extended nipples that strained in the chill air. With her arms at her side the girl looked directly into Brett's eyes.

Brett didn't let her gaze drop. "I said to take your clothes off. All of them."

Those lusciously long-fingered hands dropped to the fly of her jeans. Each button came undone, one by one. The jeans were dropped and kicked to one side, as was her underwear, so that she stood buck-naked in front of Brett.

Brett walked around her, slowly assessing every inch of her, from her well-defined collarbone to her breasts and smooth stomach to the dark patch of hair tucked between her long, long legs — legs Brett could imagine wrapped around her neck. She was gorgeous and would bring the men in by herds — but she was underage.

That was when she noticed a few marks along the woman's back: almost healed scars. Scars left by a terrible beating, probably from a while ago. She ran a fingertip down one of them and the woman shuddered. Brett knew the shudder wasn't because her finger was cold, or because her touch tickled. She knew it was what the scars meant to the girl, how she got them.

She faced the woman and looked deep into her eyes. She was too young to be here, too young to be out on the streets, alone. Brett knew all too well what she'd have to do if she didn't give her a job. She wanted to pull this girl into her arms, touch her, but not in a sexual sense. She wanted to comfort her, because she knew where the girl had been, what had been done to her. She knew this because she had been through the same thing.

"Do you have a costume?" Brett asked. Trembling, the woman shook her head. Again she looked into the woman's eyes. They were a maelstrom of emotions. There was fear and behind it was shyness and then ambition and hatred and . . . love and hope. "What's your name?" she finally asked.

"Pamela . . . Just Pamela."

"I won't turn you in. I already know you're underage. What's your name?"

"Pamela." She paused, as if assessing Brett. "Nelson."

"Is it safe to assume you don't have any music?" The woman nodded her head. "Get dressed and go out to the auditorium. I'll put some music on — you need to audition." They had just enough time to do this before the theater opened for the day.

6

Everything seemed to be more intense than it should have been and had a curious feeling of déjà vu. It didn't seem quite real and the room seemed to be changing, slowly melting into something else.

The next thing she knew she was sitting in the theater on an old, cracked vinyl seat. Music was pouring in through the speakers. It was dark except for a single spotlight on Pamela, who was on-stage, standing and looking at the floor, breathing deeply. Slowly, her body began to move, swaying to the music.

She looked out at the theater, but Brett knew her eyes were seeing nothing. Pamela wasn't really there as her hips went from side to side, as she dropped the army jacket, as she began to unbutton her shirt, leaving only one button done as she untucked it and took off her shoes. The sliver of flesh bordered on either side by those tantalizing breasts was mesmerizing. Brett wanted to see more.

Pamela started to take control of the song. The girl could dance. She turned around and looked out over her shoulder with those dark eyes. She turned back around and took off her jeans, teasing Brett by slowly pushing them down, all the while still dancing, moving to the beat that pulsed through the almost dark auditorium.

Brett noticed, uneasily, that she was shifting in her seat. Watching women dance never affected her like this, never got her this turned on.

The song ended and Pamela made as if to put her clothing back on, but Brett cleared her throat and stripped a hundred-dollar bill off a wad in her pocket. She waved this in Pamela's direction.

Brett usually didn't audition the new dancers with lap dances, which is where they would make all of their money, but she needed to be closer to this girl. Girl, she reminded herself. She couldn't believe someone this young was having this effect on her.

Pamela looked at her. Brett could tell that she had begun to drop her wall, the wall she needed to do this sort of work, but it was just the briefest flicker that crossed her face. Suddenly, she was again the dancer, the woman Brett had just seen on-stage.

Brett was now the prey and she was the hunter, slowly advancing on her. Still naked, Pamela straddled Brett's lap, and moved her shoulders, hips and groin to the music that played on. She pushed her breasts up to Brett's face, but Brett somehow managed to keep her hands on the armrests.

Brett wanted to touch her, to feel those breasts. She wanted to slide her fingers through the wetness between Pamela's legs, to feel the woman, to be inside this woman.

Instead, she reached up and ran her hand through Pamela's hair. Although it was dirty, it still felt silky. She leaned forward, about to kiss her, but the girl hesitated. Brett could almost see the wall shatter when she looked into her eyes.

Brett wasn't used to a woman hesitating when she was about to kiss her. She leaned back in her chair. "How old are you really?"

The girl paused, trying to pull her legs together and cover her breasts. "Sixteen," she finally said.

Brett rested her hands on the outside of the girl's thighs. "From now on your name's Storm and you're eighteen. I'll get appropriate ID for you." The girl looked at her. "My name's Brett, Brett Higgins. Now get dressed. I'm gonna get you a shower, a good meal and a costume, and you'll start work tonight."

Storm started to get up but then sat back on Brett's muscular thighs. Her eyes said she was scared, but she leaned forward, toward Brett, and brushed her parted lips against Brett's. Her lips were incredibly soft and there was something almost shy about the kiss, which Brett gently returned.

Without opening her eyes Storm leaned against Brett's shoulder and Brett held her shaking body, slowly stroking her back and hair until the trembling subsided.

Still holding her, Brett whispered in her ear. "It's okay, I'll take care of you. If you ever have a problem, just come to me." She couldn't believe she was saying this.

Storm nodded against her shoulder and said, her voice like a little girl's, "Okay."

"And know that the only strings attached are no tricks and no drugs. I don't want you out on the streets."

Storm lifted herself from Brett's shoulder. She looked into Brett's eyes and Brett knew, inexplicably, that her wall was down further at that moment than it had been in years.

This time when Storm kissed her, she wasn't shaking.

When she awoke, Brett was covered in sweat and trembling from head to toe. She glanced over at Allie, who lay sleeping peacefully beside her.

Storm was dead, had been dead for over five years, but Brett felt as if the beautiful woman had just been in her arms, had just been there with her. Her heart ached as she kept telling herself that Storm was indeed dead, but every time she closed her eyes she saw the long, thick black hair, the deep eyes, the sensuous lips . . .

Brett rolled onto her back, away from Allie, and stared at the ceiling. She was trying not to think of herself as Brett Higgins because that was a bit of her past that was best left dead. There were far too many people far too happy to see Brett Higgins dead and buried, too many people with too many grudges against her.

She missed the excitement of her old life, missed going out and recruiting dancers, ordering and negotiating items for the bookstores to sell, always having to be on the alert in case their competitors or the fuzz were watching her, and she missed walking through the theater and having the naked dancers walk up to her and flirt with her.

She hadn't had any of that for over a year now. It had been over a year since Allie had walked back into her life after a five-year hiatus — an event that set a strange series of events into motion, events that left almost everyone thinking that Brett Higgins was dead. She and Allie decided then that this was for the best, so Brett had changed her name to Samantha Peterson and the two went on the lam and left Detroit.

She quietly got out of bed, trying not to wake Allie as she slipped on her robe. She padded gently out of the bedroom and turned on the living room light. Pouring herself a Glenfiddich single-malt scotch on the rocks, Brett turned a chair so she could look out the window, although there was nothing to look at. The skyline in Lansing was virtually nonexistent. It was the capital of Michigan, yet it wasn't even one of the state's biggest cities. She sighed when she thought about how small this town was and that the town to which they were heading was just a speck compared to it.

She reached over to the pack of cigarettes, then changed her mind and got up to get her pipe. The long, slender curves of the handcrafted, deeply tanned, long-throated wooden pipe felt right in her hands, the way her fingers just fit around the bowl. Frankie had gotten her the Savinelli pipe in Italy after one of his semi-annual trips there.

Brett gently packed some Dunhill Elizabethan tobacco into the bowl, tamped it down with her middle finger and carefully added a bit more, rotating the flame from her Zippo over it while drawing in deep gentle puffs. She let the flame burn on after the pipe was lit, enjoying the way it danced in the breath of heat coming from the vent.

She sat back in her chair, pulling on the pipe while staring out the window and thought about the dream . . .

She had taken Storm out to her car — she smiled as she remembered that black Probe — and quickly drove up to a little lingerie shop in Clawson, where she picked out some items for Storm to use as a costume: fishnet stockings, a couple of g-strings, red spike-heeled shoes and a seductive tight red dress. As an afterthought she tossed in a few pieces of lingerie.

After she had done that, she suddenly knew what Storm was thinking — that Brett bought those for her own pleasure. Especially when they pulled up in front

11

of Brett's neat two-story house in Warren, Storm was probably figuring Brett wanted her as her own, personal sex slave.

But Brett had led her right to the bathroom. "There's the shower. Towels are in the cupboard." She quickly assessed Storm's raggedy attire. "Throw your clothes in the trash. I'll find you something else to wear."

Even though Brett's clothes were too big for Storm — Brett was about six inches taller — she looked much more at ease in the clothes Brett had found for her: jeans and a white T-shirt with a comfortable flannel shirt. She ate the hamburgers and macaroni and cheese Brett prepared as if she hadn't eaten in a long time.

That night, at the theater, she was a success. After the show Brett again brought her home, although she had never before brought a dancer to her home, let alone had one spend the night. Storm insisted she couldn't take Brett's bed, so Storm went to sleep on the couch.

In the middle of the night Brett felt someone else in the room with her. She sat up and Storm came over to sit on the edge of the bed. Even in the dim light that filtered in through the blinds she was beautiful.

"I didn't mean to wake you," Storm said. "I just needed to be near somebody. Hear you breathing." She was all but swimming in Brett's sweatpants and T-shirt.

"I'm a light sleeper. Gotta be that way in this profession."

"Why are you being so nice to me?" It was abrupt. Brett knew that was what was keeping her awake.

12

Brett thought about telling her that she knew Storm would more than make up for any expenses because of how many men she'd pull into the theater, but instead she told the truth. "Because I like you." Storm looked at her, then reached down to pull off her T-shirt. Brett stopped her. "I said I liked you, not that I wanted to sleep with you."

"Don't you find me attractive?"

"I think you're incredibly beautiful. But our deal is no drugs and no johns, not that you have to fuck me."

Storm pulled her legs up onto the bed and rested her chin and arms on them. It took Brett a few moments to realize she was crying. She pulled her into her arms, holding her and gently stroking her hair and back. She had known the girl less then twenty-four hours and already she felt protective of her, she wanted to help her. She didn't want anyone to ever hurt her again.

A few minutes later Storm stopped crying. Brett lay down with Storm curled into her, she could feel the girl's breath warm against her neck.

"Brett?" Storm said. "Thank you for the flowers." Brett had given her a dozen red roses after the show.

Brett raised herself up on her elbows so she could look at Storm, knowing the girl wanted to say something else.

Storm's dark hair was spread out over the pillow like a halo. Her face was still slightly red from the crying, and her lips and eyes were a bit puffy. Brett gently touched her own lips to Storm's.

The kiss was gentle and this time Storm wrapped her arms around Brett and pulled her to her. After the kiss, they lay inches apart and looked into each other's eyes.

Brett felt a feeling that was both familiar and unfamiliar. In her life she had fucked dozens of women, but she had never before felt like this. She wanted to make love to Storm. She knew Storm had probably been fucked hundreds of times herself, but had never been made love to.

And now she lay in Brett's arms, her body soft against Brett's, her eyelashes tickling Brett's neck, with her arms around Brett. Brett could feel her own heart quicken, her own body tense.

"Brett?" Storm said softly. "Look at me."

Never before had anyone looked at Brett like Storm did that night. It was as if Storm didn't merely look at her, but into her, as if she suddenly knew all of Brett's past and her well-buried secrets. A large part of Brett wanted to jump up, run from her, get out of the house, but instead she kissed Storm.

Brett had never before loved someone as gently as she did that night, and every night that week, until they found Storm a place of her own. But Brett would always remember Storm as her first true love and as the first person to love Brett back.

Now she loved Allie and never wanted to lose her again. In some ways it seemed that she was doomed to be a free spirit, both personally and professionally, so that she'd never be happy with a staid, stable, predictable life. Neither personally nor professionally.

Since she and Allie had gone on the lam she had tried to grow accustomed to the name Sam Peterson, which was on all her credit cards, her driver's license and all her U.S. bank accounts. Although she had substantial assets sitting across the ocean in a Swiss bank under her real name, she had fully built the identity of Sam Peterson, complete with a credit rating.

At the time she created the illusion of Brett Higgins' death, she'd had a will that left all her possessions and regular bank accounts to Allie and her old business partner, Frankie Lorenzini. Frankie actually paid her for her half of the business and took care of selling both her house and Allie's. That chunk of cash was subsequently divided between their American accounts — half in her name, half in Allie's.

Frankie was a real friend. When she and Allie decided, after a year of wandering California looking for a new place to live, to return to their real home, Michigan, he helped them get through Detroit in the quickest and most efficient way possible so they had little risk of being noticed by anyone who thought Brett was dead.

So here she was, sitting in a hotel in Lansing, Michigan — the "Middle of the Mitten." She and Allie had decided to spend the night on their way up to Alma, a little town two hours north of Detroit, because they had already spent the day traveling from California to Detroit and driving this far. They had randomly decided on Alma as their new home town.

She wished she could be back in Detroit, where her real home was. She had always said she didn't like Michigan's icy, snowy, biting winters. Said she wanted a place where you didn't go through all four seasons in a single day. But now she knew she wanted something she could be sure of, because her life was so uncertain as it was. At least Alma was closer to home than California had been.

But Sam still had a problem about her name. Her

real name was Brett Higgins, a name she had had to wait close to five years for. Brett Higgins, no middle name, no middle initial. Her folks couldn't be bothered. When she was born, Dave Higgins had told his wife Alice to come up with a name for the kid, so she remained "the kid" until the fact that she would soon begin kindergarten slowly seeped into the battered and beaten brain cells of Alice's mind and she decided the little girl she never wanted would be called Brett.

And now at twenty-eight Brett Higgins could no longer use her own long-awaited name. She looked across the room and into the mirror, studying the image that greeted her: short black hair streaked with gray from a life fraught with danger and adventure, a stern jaw and green eyes that had not only seen her kill, but had also witnessed the deaths of a lover and a friend. Even after a year of easy living her 5'10" frame was still muscular, with broad shoulders that made buying men's clothes an absolute necessity, although she would've bought them anyway.

"Sam Peterson," she addressed the mirror. It didn't fit. "Higgins, Brett Higgins," she said, and then she greeted herself with a quick, self-assured grin. She felt as if she should order a martini, "shaken, not stirred."

She was a master at playing the game, so she could do this. But sometime, she didn't know when or how, she'd be herself again.

CHAPTER TWO

"Um, Allie?" Brett asked as she glanced around at the vivid display Mother Nature was putting on. "Are we lost yet?" Even the freeways were lined with trees producing the most incredible display of colors she had seen in quite a while — red and orange and yellow, with every combination in between. All of this was highlighted with pines and spruces that refused to shed their coats during the heat of summer or the dead of winter. Even the billboards that speckled the landscape like so many little exclamation marks didn't discount her excitement at the beauty of it all. It felt good to be home.

Allie briefly consulted her map before snuggling over next to Brett, who was driving. "No, hon, not yet."

Brett wrapped an arm around Allie's shoulder while still paying close attention to both the road and the scenery. "Y'know, some people might consider sticking a state map on a wall and throwing a dart at it a really silly way of deciding where to move to." She paused. "Hi, I'm from Alma," Brett said, testing it out. "I'm an Almanian, an Almond, a regular nut."

"Home . . ." Allie said, a slight smile crossing her face.

On US-27 they noticed a billboard for Alma, declaring it the home of Alma College and the Michigan Masonic Home, as well as Little Scotland, USA.

"There's gotta be a mistake," Brett said upon seeing the sign. "We can't be going to someplace called 'Lil' Scotland' . . . What do they do there — wear kilts twenty-four/seven?"

"It can't be that bad . . ."

"Why am I suddenly getting really scared?"

"Just keep driving . . ."

"I wonder if they walk around with hayseeds stuck in their teeth and call their kids Bobby-Joe and Betty-Sue?"

"It's a small town, Brett, not the deep South."

The fields grew more frequent, the billboards slowly disappeared. Instead small, home-made signs read, "Pick your own Apples," "Fresh Produce," "Fresh Strawberries," and so on — you could find fresh almost anything out here, even pick-your-own.

Brett wondered if there was a "Pick your own Snowballs" sign once winter set in.

When they pulled off the freeway at the Alma exit, into the booming metro with its total population amounting to less than the number of freshmen at Brett's alma mater, Michigan State University, she saw the cornfields, dirt parking lots and a sign pointing to south 27.

"Are we sure we want to do this?" she asked hesitantly, overwhelmed by the lack of buildings, although there was at least one stoplight right ahead of them. Allie smirked at her, so she slowly continued forward. "What *is* that smell?" Brett asked as she quickly turned the vent off.

Allie sniffed. "Okay, so maybe you were right, maybe we don't want to do this."

They entered the town proper, and Brett discovered the reason for the awful smell of 10,000 pissed-off skunks: A refinery, with its small buildings and huge stacks spiraling toward the sky, spewing forth noxious fumes. Thankfully, however, once they were past the plant the smell eased off.

A sign welcomed them to Alma, Little Scotland, USA and proudly announced that they hosted the Kiwanis, Elks, Lions and two dozen other clubs. Then they hit the old downtown area of the city, with its quaint little shops, seeming for all the world like a small downtown Royal Oak or Birmingham, which were suburbs of Detroit. Although the street they were now on was called Superior, Brett felt it should've just been named Main Street.

Because the area was so small, they had no problems finding the realty office Frankie had told them about. They set up an appointment to go house-hunting with Ted, one of the realtors, in two hours, and got directions to the Best Western on the edge of town. En route to the motel they went through the new downtown area, a single strip lined with McDonald's, Burger King, Taco Bell, Arby's, a couple of banks, a strip mall with a JCPenney, video rental place, Rite Aid and an Ashcraft's Market, which appeared to be where most of Alma did their grocery shopping. All in all, it looked as if Alma had everything needed for basic living in the mid-1990s.

But there wasn't a single adult bookstore or theater, or anything queer for that matter, anywhere in sight. Brett sighed.

"So, girls, what price range are we looking at today?" Ted asked later that morning. To his credit, however, he didn't seem too surprised that they were looking to buy a place together.

"Whatever," Brett replied, letting the "girls" remark slide, even as she wondered if they were the only queers in town.

"We've got places all the way up to a half-mil."

"Look, Teddy boy, we've been traveling for over a year now — I just want to find a place to call home." Brett knew they had a lot of money readily accessible.

He looked at them in disbelief, but began their tour with the best Alma had to offer: the half-million-dollar homes on the city's outskirts. Some of these had tennis courts and built-in swimming pools, but none felt quite right. Through the rest of that day and the next, they slowly worked their way down the scale, all the way down to a $10,000 one-bedroom home that back in Warren or Sterling Heights would've cost at least $70,000.

During their search Ted also gave them a tour of Alma, apparently wanting to sell them on the town as well as a particular house. She had to admire this attention to detail, although to her dismay she realized some of her old persona was slipping in through the cracks — like, when he showed her the Girl Scout Cabin, which was only used during the summer, she thought that if you dumped a body there in the late fall, it wouldn't be discovered for at least six months. Of course, maybe the fairgrounds would be the better bet, because it looked as if those were only used for a bit during the summer for the annual fair . . .

Brett and Allie decided they both preferred the homes in the $50,000–$70,000 range, which were located in nice enough neighborhoods with lots of trees, because they were slightly older and had more character. But still, none seemed quite right, until . . .

"I'm sorry, but that's just about everything," Ted said as he drove them back up through a neighborhood on the second day. Brett knew the town was small, but couldn't believe they had looked at everything in less than two days.

"Wait a minute!" Brett yelled from the backseat as she jumped forward. Ted, shocked, slammed on the brakes, the car veering to the side. "That street we just passed — you didn't show us that one."

"I didn't think you'd be interested," Ted said doubtfully as he turned the car around.

The house was quaint, with white siding, an ivy-covered trellis and a covered front porch. It seemed to Brett the only thing missing was a white picket fence. She grinned when she remembered once telling a friend that she wanted it all, including a fucking white picket fence.

Allie got out of the car, looked around and smiled.

"The last people who lived here," Ted said as he led them up the leaf-covered front walk and unlocked the door, "had to move suddenly — but not before they had all new plumbing and electrical installed. And the basic structure is as sound as the day it was built," he added, thumping a wall for emphasis. He was falling back into his real estate persona.

As Ted eagerly began to show Allie the three bedrooms, two baths, spacious living room, basement and anything else he could think of, Brett examined the grounds and exterior.

Although there was something indescribable about the house, she wasn't that impressed with what she saw. But when she entered the foyer, she felt a warm breeze embrace her. It was at that moment she realized this was her home.

"Most people round here don't even bother locking their doors," Ted said as he escorted them out an hour later.

"How much?" Brett asked frankly.

"How much?" Ted replied, amazed.

"Yeah, what're they asking for it?" she repeated, wondering why this fellow was so amazed.

"Fifty."

"Fifty?" Brett asked, trying her best to hide her amazement while looking at Allie, who smiled and nodded. This house would cost two to four times as much back down where they had lived before.

Brett looked up at the house and nodded too. She thought of the warm embrace and knew in her heart that they belonged there.

"I've been told they needed to leave in a hurry, and they just want to sell. It just got listed a week ago," Ted hurriedly explained, trying to cover his surprise.

"Bullshit," came a woman's voice from behind them. Brett whipped around to find a slightly plump woman who barely reached Brett's chin standing behind her. With a rake in one hand, she wore spectacles, sweatpants, thick socks with Birkenstocks, and a Red Wings' jersey, which clashed with her wavy red hair, over a thick sweatshirt. Brett wondered if this was some strange tribal apparel.

Ted rolled his eyes heavenward.

"Madeline Jameson," the woman said, shaking first Brett's then Allie's hands. "And don't believe a word Theodore says. This house has been listed for over two years now."

"Is there something wrong with it?" Allie asked.

"No, not at all," Madeline replied. "Just be careful of Teddy here," she continued, reaching up to ruffle his hair. "He'll try to get more out of you than he should, on account of you're so obviously out-of-towners." The look she shot Brett wasn't defiant, but rather the look of someone so sure of herself she need not make a point of it.

Brett turned to Teddy. "Offer them forty —"

"Now, I know they'll never —"

"Cash. But we want to close tomorrow. I'm tired of living in hotels."

"You wanna buy a house with cash?"

"Ted, close your mouth or have a Tic Tac," Madeline said. "As for you two," she added, looking at Brett and Allie. "Would you care for a home-cooked meal with your new neighbor?"

23

"That sounds wonderful," Allie said before anyone else had a chance to say anything.

"We're having Wheatball Stroganoff with pita bread and hummus. And we'll eat all the sooner if you two will help me with the raking. It looks like the goddamned tree puked all over the lawn." With that, she turned and walked back to her own house.

Brett had spent years dealing with killers, drug dealers, money launderers and prostitutes, but already she knew that Madeline Jameson had far more power in her tiny body than any of the former could ever dream of.

"I'll see what I can do," Ted managed to croak out.

Madeline turned and looked at him. "If I were you, I'd just start drawing up the papers, because they'll accept that offer."

Later that evening, her stomach full — surprisingly enough because she usually didn't like vegetarian meals — and a cup of steaming espresso in her hand, Brett leaned against the doorway to stare at Allie, who, with Madeline, leaned over a map spread out on the table.

Allie had a way with clothes, she liked jeans just tight enough to show off her hips and legs, or dress slacks in particular fabrics that were cut in such a way as to have a nice drape as they flowed down her body. She preferred simple but tasteful blouses. In the heat of California she had worn shorts, but not jean shorts, and short-sleeved blouses of a variety of patterns. Now she wore a silk turtleneck under a thick hand-woven sweater and jeans, with low-cut boots.

Brett suspected some of how Allie dressed was based on what she knew Brett liked. Brett smiled when she thought of how many little things Allie did to please her — from the light make-up, to her perfume (Eternity), to the fact that she wore front clasp bras for "easy accessibility."

Once again Brett wondered what she had ever done to be so lucky as to win Allie's heart.

Allie flipped her long, wavy blonde hair back over her shoulder before glancing up to catch Brett staring. "Madeline's showing me some of the highlights of Alma."

"I'm just not sure if I'm a small town kinda gal," Brett said with a half-smirk. While they were still in California, Allie had convinced her that perhaps they should take a step back from big-city boisterousness; she was still hesitant about whether or not she was ready to slow down this much yet. She knew she had said she wanted a quiet life, but she wasn't sure if she was ready for it.

"I think it's the only way I'm gonna keep you outta trouble," Allie said.

"And just what type of trouble are you particularly worried about?" Madeline asked, trying for the umpteenth time that evening to discover more about her new neighbors than they were willing to share.

"Oh, nothing in particular," Brett said quickly with a grin. "I'm just an all-round sort of troublemaker." They had spent quite a bit of time while they were in California developing the story of their lives in order

25

to keep Brett's true identity a secret. Now they even kept most of Allie's past a mystery as well, partly out of habit and partly to avoid further questions.

"If you spend your lives never telling anyone anything," Madeline began, "your friends will not know how to help you when you need it."

"Who says we'll need help?"

"One of these days you're going to pull that gun on someone who has a bigger one," Allie said, not entirely convinced with Brett's apparent bravado.

"That's where the fun is," Brett replied, trying to appear casual. "In determining just how well-equipped one's opponent is."

"Nonetheless," Madeline interrupted. "I agree with Allie. Samantha, dear, you cannot go through life threatening anyone who annoys you."

"Why?"

"It's like trying to convince a man to stop peeing on the floor," Allie said. "I've been trying to change her for years."

"How long have you two been together?" Madeline asked. It had come out almost immediately that Brett and Allie were a couple, and Madeline, an English and Women's Studies professor at the college, hadn't minded in the least — in fact, she was all in favor of more queers coming to her little burg.

"All told, about two years," Brett replied.

"But we first met back in 'ninety," Allie added.

Madeline sat back and considered them. "One of these days, you will tell me everything."

"But there's nothing to tell," Brett lied. Allie also avoided looking at Madeline.

"Dear hearts, it is quite obvious that there are more than a few skeletons in your closets."

"But I burned the closet, Madeline!" Brett retorted. Throughout the evening her liking for Madeline had managed to increase dramatically, which was unusual for Brett, who was naturally suspicious of everyone and everything.

Madeline sat back and smirked. "You really are quite good at changing the subject when it suits you, Sam."

"Speaking of changing the subject," Allie said. "I've been dying to know, well, you don't really seem like the sort to be a hockey fan, so what's up with the jersey?" Madeline was still wearing the Red Wings' jersey that clashed with her hair.

"Hockey really isn't that bad, in fact, it's much more exciting than most professional sports. But no, I'm not what you'd generally refer to as a fan — I just figured I'd get on the wagon at the top of the season."

"Huh?"

Madeline shrugged as if the answer were self-evident. "The Wings will bring home Stanley this June for the first time since — why, since before either of you were born."

Brett stared at her for a moment. Then, trying to maintain her straightest, most dignified face, she asked, "And . . . is there any particular significance to the fact you're wearing number twenty-five?" People often picked one of the team's most popular players, like Wayne Gretzky, to put on their bodies.

"Of course. Darren McCarty will be shooting the winning goal." She sat back and stared at Brett, who was trying her best not to burst out laughing, before concluding with a smirk, "In case you haven't figured it out yet, I'm the town kook."

It took Brett and Allie nearly eight months to discover that Madeline wasn't quite as crazy as she first appeared.

CHAPTER THREE

"Look at this," Brett called to Allie, who was in the kitchen. Allie walked over to where Brett was kneeling in the living room. She had pulled up a corner of the carpeting and was studying the floor underneath. "Hardwood floors, covered with shitty carpeting. I love hardwood floors."

"That's nice, dear," Allie said, looking around. "Have you seen my notebook anywhere?"

"Didn't you leave it in the bedroom?"

"That's right," Allie replied, going upstairs. They had spent the day going through the house, trying to formulate a game plan. It definitely needed a thorough cleaning, dust had caked the walls and surfaces during its two uninhabited years, as well as a total repainting. They had decided the upstairs, which contained a master bedroom, a full bath and two other rooms would be their room, a guest room and Allie's room. The main floor had a living room, kitchen, half bath and another room that would be Brett's study. Although the basement wasn't finished, it appeared to be adequately sealed since they couldn't find any signs of water damage or cracking. Brett's workout equipment and the laundry area would be set-up there.

They were hoping to have contractors in soon to do most of the work while they shopped for furniture. Frankie was shipping their stuff from Detroit, but Brett figured they would still have to redecorate and buy new furniture in order to do it right. The extra cost was especially justified since the house cost less than a quarter of what they sold Allie's house for.

"Brett, did you check the pipes?" Allie asked, entering with her notebook.

"No, why?" Brett asked, looking up from her corner.

"Are you sure?"

"Allie, I know about as much about pipes as you do about the manufacturing process of Tootsie Pops."

"Well, somebody crossed 'Check Pipes' off my list," Allie said, showing her notebook to Brett. "Check Pipes" was crossed out, and next to it was written "Pipes Okay."

Brett looked up at Allie. "Maybe Madeline got some really strong vibes about the condition of our plumbing," she said, referring to Madeline's supposed psychic prowess. During the past few days, while they closed on the house and tried to make it livable, by getting the utilities hooked up and the phone turned on, they had, at Madeline's insistence, stayed in her spare room. Brett had preferred this to staying even longer at another despicable motel.

Brett really liked Madeline, but sometimes she seemed a few eggs short of an omelet. What really made Brett uneasy, however, was her ability to see through easy charades — like when she asked what Brett's real name was. Somehow she knew it wasn't Samantha Peterson.

Brett tried to tell herself her response was based on pure habit, but that wasn't it, it was something in the way Madeline met her eyes, looked into her. It gave her chills and made the breath catch in her throat, but she suddenly realized she couldn't lie to the woman.

Maybe if Rick DeSilva, Brett's old boss, was supposed to have been her father, Madeline should have been her mother . . .

"You shouldn't make fun of her like that," Allie said, pulling Brett out of her reverie.

"Y'know I like her, but I think she just might be a few tacos short of a picnic." Either that or her picnic was made of falafel and hummus, so Brett just didn't know what to make of her.

"That leaves me with one question: Do we need to have the pipes checked?"

"Yes."

"Okay, fine." Allie took the pen and wrote "Check Pipes" on her list.

"Allie," Brett began. "Do ya think we did the right thing?" She was beginning to feel a bit nervous about how fast everything was happening. Too much seemed too easy. Plus, she noticed that Allie shivered whenever she entered the house, and not only did Brett not feel the chill, but they also couldn't find out where the draft even came from.

"Of course we did," Allie reassured Brett.

"But there's so much to do."

"But when we're done, we'll be home at last," Allie replied, embracing her.

Brett smiled and held Allie tight. "We still have to de-virginate this place, you know," she teased.

"Ooh, the things you say. You just might turn a girl's head."

" 'Might'?"

Allie smiled and kissed her.

As Allie set to work on the phone, trying to line up inspectors, contractors and bidding, Brett went to investigate the rest of the house. They were in a constant state of negotiation with each other as to the exact decor. Allie finally let Brett have her way with the study; it was to be paneled in wood with shelves installed to fully cover one wall. The rest of the house was to be painted in variations of cream tones. Brett wanted some of the floors left alone, but Allie definitely wanted the entire second floor carpeted, except for the bathrooms, whose tile seemed to be in reasonable shape still.

Brett decided to take a look at the attic. It seemed logical to thoroughly inspect the house from top to bottom. She went into the upstairs hall, jumped up and grabbed the latch to the attic. She had to duck to escape being hit with the stairs that flew down at her. She made a mental note of the potential hazard.

The large attic, which was just a bit smaller than

the upper level of the house, was dusty, gloomy and made her choke and wheeze. Illuminated by two large windows at either end, it didn't appear to have any additional lighting. Mere dust bunnies didn't dare venture here — this place was instead inhabited by dust dinosaurs that lurked in the pools of light and in front of, behind and to the side of every piece of furniture or box up there. A large oak bureau sat next to a vanity with a wardrobe across from it. Old clothes lay in boxes stacked against the wall.

She was amazed at the age of the items and wondered where they came from. She couldn't believe prior owners would've simply left their stuff there, let alone that the realty company hadn't cleaned it out either.

She took off her flannel shirt, under which she wore a white T-shirt, and went downstairs for a dustpan and broom, setting to work sweeping up a majority of the dust and dirt that encrusted the floor. Once she had the spaces cleared, she emptied a corner of the room, determining that to be the junk area. Allie came up and looked around.

"Hon, write down that we need to look at the stairwell up here," Brett said.

"I would if I could find my notebook."

"It's probably where you left it."

"I left it in the kitchen, and it's not there."

Brett shook her head and went down, with Allie close behind. She methodically went through room by room until she found the notebook in the study. She handed it to Allie.

"I haven't been here since this morning," Allie insisted when Brett glared at her.

"You must've been."

"No, we finished discussing the study this morning."

"Okay. Fine. So it's a possessed notebook." She had never known Allie to be so flaky. People who misplaced things were one thing, people who needed help finding them were another, and people who insisted they never left the things where they had were in a class all by themselves.

"Samantha Peterson," Allie said, putting her arms around Brett's neck. "You are being an A-one grouch today."

"Am not."

"You are and don't even try to deny it."

"There's just so much work to do around here . . ."

"I know, and it'll get done, but we won't get any done if we spend all our time arguing about pipes and notebooks."

Brett realized the truth in this and kissed Allie. "I love you."

"Now, about the attic," Allie said as she led the way back upstairs.

"I think we should pull everything down . . ." Brett began.

"Why? We might want to keep some of it — and if it's up there, it won't be in anybody's way."

"If we're not gonna use it, we should either give it away or throw it away. We'll have enough of our own crap to put up there —" Brett stopped as she entered the attic. A little light by the bureau was on. A little light she had not noticed previously.

"Did you turn on that light?" she asked Allie.

"No, you must've done it."

"I didn't do it."

"And I didn't leave the notebook in the study. So what do you make of this?"

"You're a smart ass," Brett responded, approaching Allie.

"Better'n being a dumb ass," Allie replied, putting her arms around Brett's neck. Brett looked at her, knitted her brow and walked over to examine the light.

"There must be a short or something . . ." Brett began, examining the light and its cord. She pulled the cord out of the wall. "Might be a fire hazard."

"But now we're in the dark." The sun was going down. "Don't take your frustration out on inanimate objects."

Brett reluctantly plugged the light back in and looked about the room. "What a mess!" she said, shaking her head. "Did you have any luck with the contractors?"

"It's the strangest thing," Allie began.

"What, hon?"

"A few of the local people told me they were overbooked when I told them the address."

"Fine. We'll get someone from Lansing."

"I just can't imagine a town this size keeping somebody that busy."

"Fuck 'em. In a town this size it's probably 'cause we're strangers."

"Will you look at this thing?" Allie said, shrugging and indicating the bureau. "It's gorgeous."

"Solid oak, by the looks of it," Brett said, pounding the top to emphasize her statement. There was a loud thunk.

"Great! Now you've broken it. And I wanted it for our bedroom."

"It's old oak, it doesn't break," Brett said, stepping back and examining the bureau. Allie got on her knees and reached under it.

"It was this," she said, handing Brett a leatherbound book. Brett took the book and flipped it open. On the cover page, in painstakingly perfect calligraphy, was written one name: Liza. Allie stood next to her as she flipped through the pages of what was obviously a journal.

"I wonder if there's any more." Brett knelt by the bureau and reached up underneath, feeling around.

"Did you find something?" Allie asked as Brett stood and brushed her knees off.

"I'm not sure, can you give me a hand?" Brett asked, as she began to nudge the bureau away from the walls. "I want to turn it on its face."

Allie helped her pull out the drawers, which only contained a few moth balls apiece. They carefully lowered the piece onto its face so they could examine the bottom. When Brett slammed her fist on the top, she had apparently knocked loose a clumsily fitted piece of wood that was meant to hold the journal and another book in their hiding place on the dresser's underside. The other book was a collection of the works of Emily Dickinson. There were several sheets of loose-leaf shoved within its pages.

Brett took the books and went to sit on a nearby trunk.

"Oh, no you don't," Allie said, taking the books and laying them on the vanity. "We have work to do."

"But, but . . ." Brett began, stopping when Allie gave her the "I mean business" stare.

"If you're not going to calm down until we get this house done, I want this house done," she said, with finality.

CHAPTER FOUR

July 19, 1966

Miss Ames, my old middle school English teacher, gave me this book to write in when I left for high school. It always seemed like far too grand of a book to write less than the most significant thoughts in, but at this rate, I'll never have any of those. Miss Ames told me I might have a future as a writer, but I'll have to work at it and write every day. She was probably just being nice to me because I'm so bad at math and science.

Jen and I went to the park today, but there was a

grasser going on, and I don't really care for weed, or the people who smoke it. Jen's got a job working at the market this summer, so hopefully she can buy a car soon so we can go hang out at the beach or something. This town is just too small.

Brett began to nod off. Damn that Nyquil anyway. Somehow she had gotten a cold, and she never got colds. She had told Allie they couldn't leave all the windows open, even while the painting was going on, but Allie did it anyway. Sometimes, she'd get up to open a window after Brett fell asleep, and that really irritated her. Maybe they should've stayed at Madeline's a bit longer, but Brett didn't feel comfortable with that option either. She didn't want to overstay her welcome, nor try Madeline's hospitality.

Tonight, Allie was in Lansing looking at furniture. Over the past few days they had had people in to do the painting, and had selected the carpeting and rugs together. All the new carpeting was now laid and they had picked up the rugs earlier in the day. It was beginning to look like a home.

Allie had wanted Brett to go with her tonight to look at furniture, but Brett told her she wasn't feeling well. The last thing she wanted to do tonight was be dragged from store to store comparing the differences in size, shape, color and texture of sofas and chairs. Anyway, she trusted Allie's taste, and the things she cared about most — her desk, chair, filing cabinet and computer — were being delivered from Detroit. Frankie had personally run up some of the really important things they needed immediately: a bed, some blankets and pillows and a box of dishes.

Regardless, she figured she could veto any of

Allie's choices if they were really atrocious. She smiled as she imagined Allie's reaction to her veto: "You're such a damned butch. You don't want to go shopping with me but you don't like anything I pick out."

But somehow, she knew she'd like all of Allie's choices. Allie had good taste and knew Brett well enough to know what Brett would and wouldn't like.

Brett sighed and fluffed her pillows a bit more. She opened Liza's journal again and began reading.

I remember the day I met Jen, we were in the same home ec class, and it was a riot. Jen is not the sort of person one would imagine cooking dinner for anybody. I thought she was kinda scary at first, with her pants and saddle shoes, but we got assigned to the same stove, so I was stuck with her. Now, I don't know what I'm gonna do when she graduates. She'll be graduating at the end of this year, and I'm stuck here for another year after that. It's times like this that I realize how much I hate my life.

Brett yawned and stretched. She had never known just how restless a sleeper Allie could be. She couldn't totally hold it against Allie, but something had to be done about it. Brett couldn't keep up on the amount of sleep she'd been getting recently, what with Allie murmuring in her sleep, and stealing the covers and opening the windows . . . Maybe she wasn't meant to spend her life with this woman. It wouldn't be so bad if she could at least decipher what Allie was saying. All she could ever make out was something about speaking or talking.

Ah, what the hell, Brett told herself, admit that you love the woman and move on. You know she won't be able to get rid of you that easily. Brett smiled to herself about this.

Allie had even, miraculously enough, seemed to understand her problem with the name. Of course, Brett noticed that even Allie had a problem referring to her as Sam, so the other day, while they were going through catalogues of carpeting and paints, selecting the new color scheme of their home, Brett had brought it up.

Allie had quickly and easily suggested they tell everyone that "Brett" was her middle name, so she, Allie, could call her by it, although it might be in their best interests if Brett did introduce herself to new people as Sam. This would help ensure that she could remain hidden.

Brett skimmed through the next several journal entries, with their mentions of fixing the hiding spot for the journal, and descriptions of Liza's mom, Margaret, her father, Carl, an auto mechanic and the town minister, and her sweet twin sister, Elise, who Liza saw as possessing all the good they had between them. She enjoyed the feeling of the old book in her hands, with its black textured leather cover and its crisp pages, lovingly written on.

September 13, 1966
Jen got her car and we took it out for a spin outside of town, then went to Pine River Park. It's so very beautiful back in the woods. We got back late, and Jen wanted to come in and tell Dad it was her fault,

but I wouldn't let her. I don't know if she knows what it's like for me at home.

Dad was waiting up for me. As expected. When he left my room, Elise came in to sleep with me and dry my tears. She never mentions what he does to me, maybe 'cause she's happy it's not her, but I am, too, because I don't think she could survive it. I know Mom can't sleep through the noise, but she never says or does anything. She always ignores the bruises and cuts and black eyes, except for the time he broke my arm.

She took me to the doctor that time, and said that I fell off a stool. That night she got into a fight with Dad.

Brett was getting pissed at Carl Swanson, the town minister. Wasn't that always the way? The religious get away with murder because no one would ever dare accuse them of any wrongdoing. He'd probably say it was his family, so what he did with it was his own damn business.

Again she thought of Storm, and the way the girl had come to her. Brett had never admitted to anyone her own abusive past, but one night Storm finally got up the courage to tell Brett her story, how she her stepfather raped and beat her and how she ran away from home and kept running away until Brett helped her stay away.

Yeah, Brett thought with a chill, she sure helped Storm, helped her get killed.

With a chill Brett realized that although she had originally empathized with Liza herself, she now thought of Liza as she had Storm. She wanted to protect her, take care of her. Of course, by now Liza was a full-grown woman, probably married with a family of her own. Brett just hoped she had stopped the chain of abuse, that she had found her way out.

She looked at her watch, got up, pulled her robe on over her white T-shirt and flannel Joe Boxer pajama bottoms and fixed herself some soup in the microwave. After she was done eating, she turned off the living room and kitchen lights and went back up to bed, pulling the afghan they had bought back in California over the comforter before she continued reading.

January 3, 1967
Jen gave me a beautiful gold locket for Christmas. I told her she shouldn't spend her hard-earned money on me, and she said she couldn't find anyone better to spend it on.

New Year's Eve Mom and Dad told me I could go to a party Jen's parents were throwing and then spend the night there. At midnight, Jen pulled me into the coat closet and kissed me.

It wasn't the sort of kiss I'm used to giving people at New Year's. We didn't have a chance to say anything before Jen's mom was pulling us out of the closet and into the room. It wasn't until 2 a.m., when everyone was leaving and we were going to bed, that we had a chance alone.

We had gone upstairs into Jen's room. I've often slept in the same bed as Elise, or lots of other girl-friends, but this was the first night I was gonna spend with Jen. Jen told me I could sleep with her or on the floor or on the couch, or she could sleep somewhere else and I could have her bed. I told her I had no problem sharing a bed with her, and she walked over and kissed me again. She told me she had wanted to do that for a long time and only hoped I felt the same.

I was nervous and scared. I've never kissed a boy even. But it felt good.

I went to look for my pajamas but Jen began to slowly unbutton my shirt. I started to tremble and cry, even though she touched me so softly and gently. I really didn't want her to stop, but it was like something just came over me and I couldn't help myself.

She pulled me into bed and held me, just held me, all night long.

I'm confused and scared and don't know what to do.

Brett tried to remember how it was to be so young and naive. So young and confused. She tried to imagine everything Liza must have been going through and thought she could empathize fairly well, having come out herself at a young age in an abusive household.

The bedside light went out. To no avail Brett jiggled the cord, switched the light off, then on again. She got up and flicked on the overhead light, but that didn't work either. They had thought the electrical system was all right, damn it. She looked outside and saw that Madeline's lights were on, so she went to the kitchen, trying to remember where the circuit breaker was. Just in front of her, on the Oriental carpet in the living room, was a body. A body that wasn't moving.

Brett stopped, stunned, but as she watched, the body got up. It seemed to be illuminated from within. It was a pretty, young girl, with long dark hair, rather pale skin and dark eyes, dressed in a simple patterned dress. Something about her created a feather-tickle within Brett's brain, like a thought not quite yet conceived.

The girl looked at her. "But who listens when the dead speak?"

CHAPTER FIVE

May 6, 1967

Jen took me to the park, deep into the woods. It was broad daylight, but nobody was around. We found a nice secluded spot and she spread out a blanket and told me there was nothing to be afraid of. I was shaking and near tears as she lay me down on the blanket. Her touches were gentle as she ran her hands over my face and through my hair. Her lips were so soft when she kissed me. Even though she's kissed me hundreds of times since that first kiss, her kisses still make my knees weak.

I knew what was coming. Since that first night we'd only touched through our clothes, but I knew today she wanted to go further.

When she unbuttoned my blouse, I was afraid that she'd be disappointed with the size of my breasts, but, instead she said that they were the most beautiful she'd ever seen. She kissed them and caressed them and ran her hair over them. For the first time in my life, they felt as if they were a part of me.

It seemed like an eternity later that I was lying naked in the shade. She was so caring I wasn't afraid. When she touched me down there I felt ready to burst. I could feel every movement of her fingers, fingers that used to seem so rough and ready for hard labor.

Everything about Jen today was soft and caring. The sun in her eyes made them seem like twinkling emeralds as she ran her hands all over my body, creating sensations I had never before thought possible. Her fingers slid in and out of me, making me want more.

She pushed back and forth and in and out, she kissed my body and ran her lips over my bare skin. Gradually, she worked her way down, until she was kissing me between my legs. Her warm breath and tongue touched me, moved back and forth over me, and I knew I was very wet, wet like I had never been before. And she kept her fingers inside me as she ran her tongue over me, and her other hand lay on my breast, and though I felt exposed in the cool air, I also felt free and wonderful.

47

I never knew anything could be like that.

Afterward, when I was lying in her arms, she told me that she loved me.

And now I know, nothing that feels this right can be wrong: I love her.

Allie pulled the book out of her hands.

"Several men are going to be bringing tons of shit here any minute and all you can do is sit there reading?" She was referring to the men hauling their stuff up from Detroit. They had found some locals to do the chore, since they wanted as few clues to their identity as possible.

"I don't feel well," Brett replied, reaching for another tissue from where she sat on the floor.

"You shouldn't've been up half the night drinking."

"I'm telling you, that was Nyquil you smelled on my breath," Brett replied, silently justifying to herself that Allie may have smelled the Nyquil, not the scotch, on her breath. She hadn't told Allie about her "vision" of the night before. She figured it was a Nyquil-induced delusion. After all, she didn't start drinking until after the lights had come back on. By then, she felt she needed a good, strong belt.

"Are you sure there isn't something you're not telling me?" Allie asked.

"Positive." There was no way she was going to tell Allie that the trail of dead bodies had followed them up to Alma.

Allie shivered and wrapped her arms around herself as she looked out the front window. "Do you sometimes get the feeling that this house doesn't seem quite right?" she asked, looking back at Brett.

48

"It's an old house, things settle, little spots let in drafts. It'll feel better once we've made it our home," Brett said, hoping the words could convince her as well.

"Whatever you say," Allie said as the doorbell rang.

"This the Sullivan-Peterson residence?" a man asked as soon as Allie opened the door. He was tall, lean, clean-shaven and in his early twenties.

"Yes, it is," she said. "You can just bring everything right in here."

"No, ma'am, I'm sorry, we can't," he began, and continued before Allie could interrupt. "It's my partner, Tom," he said, indicating the truck parked in the driveway. "He says he won't step foot in this here house."

"Why not?" Brett asked, stepping forward.

"Well, maybe you should ask him."

"Yeah, all right," Brett said, putting on her shoes. She just didn't need this today.

"I never thought he was afraid of nothin'," the man said as he led Brett and Allie out to the truck.

"Hi!" Tom said, jumping out of the truck. He was fortyish, over six feet tall, around 200 pounds. His black hair was slightly wavy and he had a short, scraggly beard. Like Steve, he was wearing jeans, heavy boots and a denim jacket over a thick flannel shirt. The two men could've been father and son.

"This is Tom," the first man said, "and I'm Steve."

"Nice to meet you," Brett said, not offering a hand. "So, Tom, what's the problem?"

"Ain't no problem," he said, looking at Brett and Allie then up at the house. "I just ain't goin' in there."

"Why not?" Brett asked, losing her patience.

"It's haunted," Tom replied.

"Haunted?" Allie asked.

"Yeah, haunted," Tom said. "Haven't you noticed that yet?"

"No . . ." Brett began. Great, the entire town is filled with wackos.

"How long you lived here?"

"We bought it a week or so ago."

"And you haven't noticed lights goin' on and off by themselves? Cold drafts? Voices in the night?"

"It's an old house — of course it might be a little drafty . . ." Brett said, even as cold stabs of fear jolted through her.

"Why do you think nobody wanted to buy it?"

"We were told it was listed for over two years, but that there wasn't anything wrong with it," Allie said.

"Who told you that?"

"Ted," Brett said.

"Who's Ted?" Steve asked.

"The real estate agent," Allie said.

"You believed a salesman?" Tom said, incredulously.

"Madeline agreed with him!"

"Madeline Jameson?" Tom laughed. "Yeah, she wouldn't think there was a thing wrong with it."

"Okay," Brett said, cutting off any further discussions. "You're not going into the house . . ." She didn't believe in ghosts. When people died they were gone the only way they weren't was in people's imaginations.

"Right," Tom said, nodding.

"I can get a lot of the smaller stuff myself," Steve offered.

"And Tom can help you get the big stuff off the truck and onto the lawn," Brett said. "I can help you get it the rest of the way."

"You sure about that?" Steve asked doubtfully, sizing Brett up.

"I'm sure," Brett said, steel in her voice.

"Yeah, that'll work," Tom said, nodding at Brett.

Brett went into the house to grab a drink while Tom and Steve started. When she went out to help Steve, Allie went with her.

"He just don't understand, he wasn't even born when it all happened," Tom griped as Steve moved the smaller boxes and crates. "I mean, I went to school with Liza and Jen . . ."

"Who're they?" Allie asked.

"You mean you really don't know?"

"What is there to know?" Brett asked, frustrated. What could've happened with Liza and Jen?

"Well, it all went down in sixty-seven," Tom said, sitting on the curb and lighting a cigarette. Allie sat next to him, carefully listening, while Brett stood nearby, leaning against a tree and watching skeptically. She didn't care what happened last night, she didn't believe in ghosts and hauntings.

"It was about this time of year, and we were all in school together," Tom continued, "but they decided to skip class. Everybody thinks they were" — he dropped his voice to a whisper — "lesbians." He took a puff on his cigarette, staring across the street.

"But what happened?" Allie prodded.

"Well, Elise, Liza's twin sister, she got nervous when Liza didn't come back for her last class, so we rushed right over after school." He paused, took another drag. "I was kinda dating Elise, she was a real sweet girl."

"Was?" Allie asked.

"She changed after the murder. She was always shy, but then she got withdrawn and, well, angry. She never talked much about what happened that day, or even what she thought happened."

"Murder? What are you talking about?" Allie asked, clearly tired of the cat-and-mouse game.

"We got here and there was blood everywhere. I mean, she was all but ripped apart. It was only in 'Nam a few years later that I ever saw anybody more ripped apart than that girl."

"Who was ripped apart?" Allie yelled.

"Liza."

"Liza was murdered?" Brett asked. It couldn't be. No. She shook her head.

"Somebody killed her and now she haunts the house," Tom continued. Brett continued shaking her head. She couldn't believe the lively, abused girl she was reading about, the naive girl who reminded her of her own late, beloved Storm, was dead. "Some say she's atoning for her sins, but I don't see what 'sins' she could be atoning for." He added, "Since the war, I've figured that as long as you're not hurtin' anybody, what does it matter?"

"But you say she's haunting the house," Brett said. Tom nodded. "But why then?"

"She's waiting for her killer to be found," Tom replied, nodding, a sureness in his voice.

"They didn't find him?"

"Nope, I don't think so. I mean, Jen's in prison for it all right, but I don't think she done it. You'd have to know Jen — she walked the walk and talked the talk, but underneath it all, she couldn't hurt a fuckin' fly."

"They arrested her?" Brett lit a cigarette as Steve approached.

"Arrested, tried and convicted her. You ask me, it was just some hippie come wandering through town stoned, looking for cash. He found her and freaked out all over the place. That's what everybody thought, at first."

"So what happened?" Allie asked again.

"They started wondering who saw Liza alive last. So they ask Elise, and Elise says they asked her to cut class with them, but Elise figured they wanted to be alone. People started wondering why, and that's when the rumors started flying. Stories of Jen becoming jealous 'cause Liza was gonna start dating some guy, unhappy love triangles, that sort of garbage."

"So Jen and Liza really were dykes?" Steve asked.

"Between you, me and the wall — yes. But I know for a fact Liza wasn't seeing no guy — those two were a match made in fucking heaven."

"How do you know this?" Brett asked, trying to piece it all together with what she was reading in the diary, while her heart raced.

"I was dating Elise, who, far as I know, was the only one knew what was up with Liza and Jen. Hell, before Elise told me, I thought they was just good friends, and I was the only one Elise told. That didn't matter none, though, when Carl Swanson got hold of the story."

"Carl Swanson?" Allie asked.

"He was the girls' daddy, and the town preacher.

He started spewing shit from his pulpit on the evils of unnatural behavior — how this woman Jennifer corrupted his little girl then killed her. The cops had no other choice but to pull Jen in for questioning and, when no better alternative popped up, charge her with murder."

"And the jury convicted her out of hate," Brett said, irritated and angry now. It was easier than dealing with the fact that Liza was dead. Her irritation was magnified because she knew Carl for the scum he was.

"You got it," Tom said.

"You ask me, it's the biggest loada shit in the world," Steve said, stomping out his cigarette. "Just some shit story some fucked-up kids came up with."

"Listen, asshole," Tom said, standing and facing Steve. "These days, ain't too much I'm afraid of. But this house spooks the shit outta me. Things happen here that ain't s'posed to be happening. Lights goin' on and off for no reason when nobody's been there for months. Windows opening and closing all by themselves . . ."

"There could be lots of reasonable explanations for all of that," Brett said.

"Yeah, but how 'bout the drafts in the living room?"

"An open window."

"Even in the middle of the summer?"

"There must be some reason."

"And if you go in, late at night, sometimes, if you listen real careful, you can hear somebody tryin' to say somethin'."

"Yeah, the pipes and floors sayin' they're old," Steve joked.

"I think," Tom interjected, "that's the real reason the Swansons finally moved."

"When did they do that?" Allie asked.

"Almost a year after the murder. They said it was because of memories, but I know different."

"How?"

"Elise. She wrote me a few times from Colorado, saying she could finally sleep again. When she was here, somebody kept opening windows and stealing her covers."

"Stealing the covers?" Brett repeated, suddenly not quite sure it was Allie who had been stealing the covers of late.

"Go figure," Tom said, putting out his cigarette and shrugging. "Makes about as much sense as the fact that everybody who goes into that house since the murder feels a cold draft."

Brett shivered and Tom took it as proof of his statement, when, really, she was thinking that everyone felt the draft — except her.

"You know, I thought I felt somethin'," Steve admitted.

CHAPTER SIX

Elizabeth Marie Swanson
(1/20/1951 – 11/13/1967)
Murdered in her home by an as-yet-unknown
assailant. She is survived by her father, mother and
sister. Services will be held Thursday at the Drobeck
Funeral Home in Alma.

Short and to the point. Liza was just 16, sweet 16, Brett thought. Then she realized, with a shiver, that Liza was killed on the day she herself was born. She began to wonder what time Liza was killed at, but decided that was just too . . . too . . . she hated to use the word, but it would be too spooky.

Brett was sitting in the backroom of the *Alma Sun*, Alma's only paper. She had come in hoping to look through their microfiche files, which were in surprisingly good condition, considering the size of the publication.

Allie was in Lansing again, checking their library for any daily news coverage of the murder. Although Alma was the biggest city in Gratiot County, which meant that none of the other cities there would be likely to have better newspapers, it was within an hour's drive of Lansing, so the *Lansing State Journal* might have mention of the murder.

Tom's remarks had made them both curious about their former, or perhaps current, housemate, as well as Jen's involvement in the case, so as soon as they were finished organizing and putting away all of the stuff that came in from Detroit, which took the rest of that day and the next, they decided to begin a little investigation of their own.

Brett slipped another sheet into the reader:

MURDER!

Alma, MI

 Even though a lot of people say we're just a backwater town, we've always liked it that way, but Alma has lost her innocence with her first murder.

 Elizabeth Marie Swanson, 16, was murdered in her own home on Tuesday. The body was discovered by her twin sister, Elise, and her friend Tom Ringer. They entered the Swanson home immediately after school to find

Elizabeth's mutilated body in the front room.
Ringer immediately called the police.

"I just didn't know what to make of it,"
Constable George McFarley said about his
arrival at the scene of the crime. "It looked like
somebody had taken a knife to her then decided
that wasn't enough, so he finished her off with
a bullet through the brain."

Lansing police were called in to help with
the investigation. Although there are no suspects
yet, speculation says it was an unknown male
who was spotted earlier in the downtown
district.

As Brett continued through the pile of microfiche,
she read with ever-increasing interest the web of
articles, editorials and summaries. Apparently, nothing
much besides Liza's murder happened that year in
Alma, so the local newspaper staff enjoyed the chance
to show their stuff, including special editions right
after the murder and during the trial.

The cause of death as reported in the *Sun*,
appeared to be multiple stab wounds, but a shot had
been fired directly to her head, apparently for good
measure. Talk about a literal overkill, Brett thought.

She carefully jotted down any important facts,
including an outline of events, in her notebook. She
then started a new page on which she noted the
names of all of the people quoted or mentioned in the
articles.

Police and townspeople originally assumed that a
wandering loner came into the Swansons' looking for
something, preferably money, to steal, found Liza
instead and, because he was probably on drugs,

freaked and killed her. But then the insinuations began, even as the trail ran cold on the out-of-towner.

MORE THAN FRIENDS?

"I never would've believed it," Gertrude Jarvis said when she discovered that her neighbor, the late Elizabeth Swanson, was involved in a lesbian love affair. *"She always seemed like such a nice kid."*

"But Jen McDonald wouldn't hurt a fly," argued Thomas Ringer, a close friend and schoolmate of the Swanson girls. *"She couldn't have done it!"*

"The devil works in mysterious ways," declared the Reverend Carl Swanson. *"But the Lord's retribution is swift and brutal."*

Martha McDonald, mother of Jennifer McDonald, declined comment.

The article went on to say that the police "suddenly" realized nothing was missing from the Swanson residence, so the thief not only freaked and killed Liza, but then took off without stealing anything.

Of course, conveniently enough, they only realized that the stranger didn't steal anything when the trail on him had grown cold.

Enter Carl Swanson, the town preacher, who began a furor from his pulpit on the evils of "unnatural behavior" and how his daughter was "corrupted by a vile woman" who only wanted to molest and recruit young girls. His sermons found especially fertile ground since the McDonalds had only recently — Brett guessed anything less than a decade was "recent" to

59

1960s Alma — moved to town. They were, in other words, still strangers.

Of course, it wasn't difficult to find boys who said they were or had dated, the beautiful Liza Swanson, thereby further fueling the lesbian outrage. And when Jen's story, "the truth and nothing but the truth," hit the papers, it was all over. No one believed she left the house as an intruder entered. No one believed Liza was still alive when Jen climbed down the icy trellis.

Jen was brought in for questioning, booked, tried, convicted and sentenced to life in prison. She was seventeen at the time. She'd been tried as an adult, due to the "unnatural" crime.

Brett glanced at the picture of Liza beside one article and gasped. With her long dark hair and sorrowful eyes, with her youth and naiveté, she looked much like Storm, the old lover Brett had been unable to save, the lover that the mysterious vision in her living room had reminded her of.

"Are you finding everything you need, dear?" Sylvia Richards asked, coming up behind Brett. From the first moment Brett entered the *Sun*'s offices, Sylvia in her polyester pastel-colored clothing made Brett feel ill-attired — but it wasn't from the way Sylvia was dressed, it was from her attitude toward Brett. Something about her reaction toward Brett made Brett suddenly realize how much she'd changed over the past year.

Back when she was still in business, Brett nearly always wore a suit, or blazer and slacks, with a shirt and tie. Quite often these latter items were silk. She very rarely ever wore jeans, except when she went to queer activities, and never wore shorts. It had taken a bit, but Allie had finally gotten her to wear a few pairs of jean shorts while they were in California. But now she mostly wore T-shirts, flannel shirts, sweaters and jeans. Always jeans. And she had exchanged her loafers and lace-ups for sneakers and boots.

Today's selection was an especially beat-up pair of Girbaud's with a rip in one knee, a white T-shirt with a flannel shirt over it and a black leather jacket with combat boots. She suddenly felt like a slob. She had thousands of dollars in clothes neatly hung in her closet, and she was dressed like this.

Of course, Sylvia probably would've reacted even more negatively to the way Brett used to dress, but it wasn't Sylvia she was concerned with, she was more concerned with the way she was letting herself go right downhill.

Brett glanced up at Sylvia and looked at her watch. "Oh, shit," she said, realizing the time and remembering that Madeline was due for dinner.

"Is everything all right?" Sylvia asked as Brett quickly gathered her notebooks and paper.

"Yeah, just forgot an appointment," Brett said, carefully collecting the microfiche to return to Sylvia, who appeared to be the *Sun*'s receptionist, bookkeeper and morgue keeper.

"If there's anything else I can do for you . . ." Sylvia offered with a smile. Apparently it didn't matter how many duties the paper gave her, she would still end up with time on her hands.

"Oh, I'm sure I'll be back."

"Do you mind my asking why the interest in the Swanson case?"

"Well, um," Brett began, trying to quickly concoct a story. "I'm a writer, and I'm thinking about basing a novel on it."

"Oh, my! How exciting! You know," she confided, "they say Liza haunts their old home . . ." She raised her eyebrows.

"Yeah, I know. That's how I found out about it — I live there." How could she get rid of this woman?

"Is it true? I mean, I knew Liza — all the Swansons in fact."

"Oh really?" asked Brett, leaning back against the counter, her interest piqued. She was surprised that Sylvia didn't already know who she was and where she lived. Maybe Alma wasn't quite as small as she had first thought.

"I worked with Carl at John's Auto."

"I thought he was a preacher?" Brett already knew, from Liza's journal, that Carl was also a mechanic, but she was hoping to find out more about why this was.

"He was, but Alma couldn't really afford a full-time minister at the time. And he was such a kind, godly man that he took no salary from the church. Said he didn't need pay to do the work of the Lord. Now look at this town — it's just filled with churches! Of course, some of them aren't the right ones, but —"

Obviously, this woman took her religion seriously, so Brett cut her off before she got a lecture on the right and wrong religions. "So he worked at John's Auto?"

"Yes. He was a very hard worker, very devoted to God, his family and his town —"

Obviously, this was a woman who was born to be

cut off. "But I understand he left town shortly after the murder."

"The memories, dear. Poor Carl may have been able to survive it, but Margaret, his wife, and Elise couldn't."

"Elise was Liza's twin?"

"Yes, and the two were always together. Until that awful Jennifer showed up, that is."

"Y'know, I've really got to run," Brett said, folding her list of names gleaned from the paper, "but I'd really like to come back and talk with you more."

"That would be fine, dear. Maybe I'll bring you some cake. Carl always loved my cake . . ." Sylvia replied, drifting off.

"You baked for him?"

"It was the least I could do, as did many of the women. We felt that if we couldn't pay him, at least we could share our meals with him and his family. After all, he worked so hard, two jobs, in order to keep his flock together in peace."

"Yes, I'm sure," replied Brett as she left.

"Brett, she's been dead for nearly thirty years, what the hell does she expect *us* to do about it?" Allie said as she and Brett flew through the kitchen trying to prepare dinner. Brett, who was rushing to the refrigerator, bumped into her.

"Honey," Brett began patiently. "Why don't you go tidy the living room and I'll finish in here?" Allie was not the sort of woman who was born to cook. If Brett was in a hurry, she preferred that Allie *not* help.

And Lord knew the place needed tidying, because although they had put away everything that had been shipped, the place was still a bit of a mess, and would be until they got all the new furniture and things Allie had bought.

"You still haven't answered my question!" Allie yelled from the living room. They had shared notes while they began dinner, although neither had very much to share that the other didn't already know. The *Lansing State Journal* did have a few editorials about the injustice of Jen's trial, but of course, being a bit larger and not almost entirely blue-collar, Lansing was a bit more liberal, even though it was still pre-Stonewall America these events had transpired in.

"How the hell should I know?" Brett responded. "And remember, I don't believe in ghosts." Perhaps unreasonably, Brett felt compelled to try to see justice done, which was a switch considering her prior career.

"Tsk, tsk, tsk. That's the problem with people these days, they don't want to believe in anything they can't see and feel," Madeline said, walking in the front door. Brett peered around the corner and saw her. Madeline suddenly stopped and looked around.

"Oops!" Brett said, shrugging nervously.

"Oh, don't worry. I always knew you were a non-believer," Madeline said, hugging Brett, even as she continued to look about. Brett sensed something was the matter.

"How have you been?" Allie asked, tossing her arms around Madeline.

"Well. Although I must admit that I am *not* looking forward to the onslaught of yet another round of final exams. But don't try to change the subject — we were talking about ghosts."

"The house is haunted," Allie said.

"It is not!" Brett retorted, slamming the oven door. The rolls were still not finished. She hated having to mess around with an unknown oven. She had finally gotten her old kitchen just the way she wanted it when she was forced to move.

"Do tell!" Madeline said, sitting on the couch and ignoring Brett. Brett returned to her cooking and left Allie to fix Madeline a drink and fill her in on the details of their research — and any of the "strange" happenings Allie felt obliged to blame on the so-called ghost.

The conversation briefly stopped when dinner was ready, but no sooner had they sat down then Madeline reintroduced the subject.

"So, Brett, you say you don't believe in ghosts, but you're taking an active interest in the life and death of Liza Swanson. Why is that?"

"Curiosity. We found her diary and I'm kinda interested in what happened to her," Brett replied as honestly as she could. She just couldn't shake her feelings about the house, though — that they were somehow meant to be there. She hated the idea that she was set up, but she had a feeling that that was about what had happened. Somehow she had been dragged from California to this house.

"But," Allie said, "the problem is, if there is a ghost, and it's Liza Swanson, what does she want us to do?"

"Should we have her exorcised or what?" Brett asked.

"Oh, no no no!" Madeline exclaimed. "If you do that, you may condemn her to an eternity of nothingness, and that would be a really bad thing."

"So what should we do?" Allie asked.

"She must have left behind unfinished business. It could be something she needed to do, or someone she was supposed to help or, as you seem to suspect, it may have to do with her death."

"But she's been dead for nearly thirty years — what does she expect us to do about it?" Allie said.

"You are the first people who have lived here to take the matter seriously enough to attempt an investigation. Everyone else who has lived here has moved out fairly quickly — within a year or two."

"Why?"

"They were scared of the ghost," Madeline replied quite frankly. "As for myself, she seems to have noticed my tendencies toward the supernatural and has, thus, for whatever reasons, never given me any indication as to her presence." Madeline glanced around, somewhat nervously it seemed, before continuing, "She must have been waiting for you two to move in here."

"I have a question," Brett said. "If so many people have lived here, why didn't anyone ever clear out the attic?"

To Madeline's questioning look Allie said, "We found some old furniture and clothing up there. That's where we found the diary."

"I heard a couple of people say they were going to look through it because they already knew they wanted some of the furniture," Madeline said, sitting back with her wine. "So I would have to guess they were afraid there was bad luck or something associated with the items. Of course, between unpacking their own possessions when they moved in and then repacking it all when they left so soon after, I'm sure

66

it could have just as easily been that no one got around to it. But, you must remember, I did not live next door when the Swansons lived here — I only moved in about fifteen years ago."

"I can understand that," Allie said. Brett thought of the entire hassle they were going through just trying to unpack everything, so she could relate to someone just putting off something like that so long that they simply decided against doing anything about it.

"Of course, as you must admit, it is quite extraordinary that these items have remained here for so long," Madeline said with a shrug. "It could be simply that Liza didn't want them to remove anything."

Brett rolled her eyes. Would this woman ever stop this shit? "So what should we do?"

"You could attempt to communicate with the spirit," Madeline said and held up her hand to stop any interruption from Brett. "To see if she gives you any direction. Or, you could continue as you are, and see what you find."

"Tom mentioned —"

"He was the moving man," Allie explained, and Madeline nodded.

"— that at first people thought the killer was some hippie vagabond who was wandering through town."

"And that may be the problem — perhaps it was, and now Liza's lover is wrongfully imprisoned for her murder."

"But it seems that the reason they questioned Jen in the first place was that they couldn't find the strange man," Allie replied.

"So you have your work cut out for you."

"Work?" Brett asked, taking the plates to the sink.

"Let's be real here. I'm curious about this girl, and about this house. But just how seriously are we gonna take this, Allie?"

"Brett, dear," Madeline replied, coming into the kitchen. "A lot of the hate and discrimination in this world is based on fear of the unknown — homophobia, for example. Many people do not understand homosexuality in others or in themselves, so they rebel against it. Elizabeth Swanson was killed and, because of this minute detail, you want to disregard her apparent wishes for fulfillment of this material life, so that she can move on. You," Madeline said, putting her hand on Brett's shoulder, "are being ghostophobic. Do not discriminate against the poor child because she is no longer with us."

"But for all we know," Brett argued, "this is an old house with strange drafts, and this is a town with an over-active rumor mill."

"Brett, dear, I didn't want to tell you this," Madeline began, "but as soon as I walked into this house I felt something. Now, I wasn't immediately sure if it was your ghost or merely you and Allie —"

"What?"

"Because the thought that passed through my soul was that someone wanted to speak."

"To speak?" Allie asked.

"I thought perhaps you two had decided to come clean with me and tell me whatever it is you've been hiding..."

"For once and for all, we haven't been hiding anything!" Brett lied, even as she felt a touch of déjà vu.

"Whatever," Madeline conceded with a wave of her hand. "But perhaps the spirit has something to say."

"Brett," Allie said, putting her arm around Brett's waist. "Maybe we shouldn't be thinking so much about helping Liza as we should about helping Jen."

"Perhaps she has a point, Brett," Madeline said. "After all, would you want to spend your life in prison for a crime you didn't commit?"

The point struck a deep cord within the heart of the woman who once was Brett Higgins, almost arrested for an array of murders perpetrated by another. "What I don't get though, Madeline," she said, "is why this all seems to be news to you. After all, you've lived next door for years."

"I never knew the Swansons, nor poor Liza, and I feel that, until summoned, such as you have been, 'tis often better to leave such things alone."

"So you knew the house was haunted when we bought it?"

"I had heard stories to the fact, but had never been a first-hand witness of such."

"Then why didn't you mention it when we asked about the house?"

"Dear heart, you asked if anything was wrong with it — and there is nothing wrong with it. It just happens to be haunted." Brett turned and faked banging her head against the wall as Madeline continued. "Furthermore, although I have been in this house over a hundred times since I moved in next door, tonight is the first time I have ever felt anything when I entered. I would assume this means that the spirit has no real interest in me, but instead has found one or both of you to be suitable for her needs."

"Huh?" Brett looked at her. This was just too unreal.

Allie pulled Brett close. "What she's saying is that now there's another woman who wants our butts."

After Madeline left, Allie finished cleaning up in the kitchen while Brett retired to the living room to continue reading the journal.

"Dinner was wonderful, honey," Allie said.

"Thanks," Brett replied, not looking up.

"For somebody who doesn't believe in ghosts, you sure are interested in that journal."

"I guess it's all kinda like living a mystery novel," Brett admitted. "The entire story has me rather intrigued."

"I just wish you'd let me know what you're really thinking."

Brett looked up as Allie disappeared down the hallway. Lately, she had been possessed with thoughts of how she might've saved Storm. How she was sure she was due some sort of retribution for the things she had done, how she was afraid of bringing Allie into it all.

"What do I have to do to get you to look at me?" Allie asked, returning to the room.

Brett shrugged, trying to bring her focus to the words on the page, trying to avoid crying. She felt Allie standing very near.

Allie reached over, took the journal from Brett's

hands and laid it on the end table. Brett finally looked up. Allie wasn't wearing anything except a diamond and gold heart necklace Brett had given her years ago.

Brett gasped as Allie straddled her legs and sat on her lap, leaning down to brush Brett's lips with her own. Brett stroked the soft smoothness of Allie's thighs, then the plushness of her breasts. Her nipples were already hard little peaks gracing the nearly white skin. She leaned forward to grab a nipple in her mouth as Allie stretched and arched to offer it to her. She held it in her teeth as her tongue played across it, teasing it until it became even larger. She cupped both Allie's breasts in her hands and brought them together, her tongue swishing back and forth across them, then she took both nipples simultaneously in her mouth.

Allie cupped her own breasts so that Brett was free to explore her naked flesh. She ran her short fingernails down Allie's back, then reached down to cradle Allie's ass. She pulled the cheeks apart and ran a finger near the opening. Allie moaned in enjoyment, arching further still so that Brett had to catch her in her arms.

"Why don't we go upstairs?" Allie said breathily. Brett picked Allie up, carried her to their bedroom and threw Allie on the bed, then quickly undressed herself.

Allie lay sprawled across the coverlet. Brett roughly grabbed her wrist and brought it up to the headboard. They had mounted ropes and wrist cuffs on all corners of the bed. Allie pretended to complain and resist as Brett roughly tied her up, spread-eagled and fully exposed.

"Damn you're beautiful," Brett said, as she stood

openly admiring Allie's long legs, full breasts, tiny waist and blond pussy. She climbed on top of Allie and pushed her own breasts between Allie's legs. Allie moaned her appreciation. "I'm gonna have you and there's not a damned thing you can do about it," she growled into her ear. Brett knew Allie enjoyed being helpless, letting Brett do whatever she wanted, giving all control to her.

Allie groaned as Brett lightly rubbed her hipbone into her crotch. When Brett put her hand on her, she knew Allie would be drenched, dripping onto the bed. She needed Brett, wanted her to touch her.

Brett rolled off her and let her fingers wander all over the contours of Allie's body, tracing intimate little patterns across her nipples, brushing her armpits, gliding over her stomach to her inner thigh, enjoying the softness of Allie's skin, and the way each touch made her groan and writhe. Brett brought her hand up to cup Allie's fur-covered lips, but still she didn't dive into the wetness. Allie moaned as she arched, trying to entice Brett into feeling her. She wanted Brett inside her.

Brett looked into Allie's eyes. "I'll do what I want." She slowly slid her finger along the side of Allie's clit and Allie shivered in anticipation. Brett's fingers danced in the wetness, sliding up and down Allie's clit, circling her vagina and pulling on the swollen flesh of her clit.

Brett got up and walked away from the bed. She wanted to push Allie, take her to new places. She needed to satisfy Allie, make her want her, need her. She carefully donned the largest of their strap-ons, tightening the leather harness around her waist and liberally applying lube to the cool, pink rubber. She approached the bed and stood beside it, looking down at Allie.

"Oh, God," Allie moaned, looking at the large tool.

"Think you can take it?" Brett mounted Allie, slowly sliding it all the way in as Allie arched to meet the challenge. Brett grabbed a nipple in her teeth as she raised herself on her arms and pulled out. Brett knew Allie's rhythms well as she slid back in, then pulled out, following Allie's lead.

Brett teased her, not going quite fast enough. She knew Allie wanted to come, needed to come, but wouldn't speed up quite enough. She wanted Allie to ride the wave a bit longer, even as Allie began to scream.

Brett brutally rode her with an ever-increasing pace, shoving the large, thick dildo all the way into her, then pulling out again, all the while teasing Allie's nipples.

Sweat covered Brett's body as she slammed in and out of Allie increasing her pace. Allie was screaming and writhing about the bed, barely able to move within the tight restraints as she flew over the edge of the wave.

After releasing Allie from the restraints, Brett snuggled with her for a bit before going down to the kitchen to get them a glass of water. Her throat felt parched, and her skin was still slightly damp as she turned the light on. She pulled the container of water from the refrigerator and was pouring it into a glass when she heard footsteps behind her. She turned to see Allie smiling, still naked and flushed from sex, leaning against a wall.

"I'll be up in a sec, babe," Brett said, returning her smile.

"I know," Allie said with a mischievous grin. "But I want you. Right here, right now."

Brett felt her knees go weak as Allie pressed her against the counter and ran her lips down her throat to her still hard nipples.

"Get up on the counter," Allie growled in a commanding way. "And spread your legs wide open."

Heat surged through Brett's belly as she looked at Allie. Allie was the only woman who had ever been able to treat Brett like this, to control Brett in such a way.

"Now," Allie said. Brett obeyed. Allie ran her hands over Brett's body, almost viciously pinching the hardened buds of her nipples. She grabbed Brett's ass and pulled Brett to the very edge of the counter. She laid her hands gently on Brett's thighs, then thrust Brett's legs farther apart.

"I want you totally exposed, with the lights on," she growled, eyeing Brett's wet cunt. Brett braced herself as Allie reached down and pulled apart the fleshy folds of skin with her thumbs.

"My God, you're wet," she said.

"Fucking you always turns me on," Brett growled back as she felt her lips become more swollen.

"I want you to spread your lips for me," Allie said, grabbing Brett's arms. Brett leaned back against the cupboards. "I want you to show me everything you've got." She put Brett's hands where she wanted them, spreading the lips open wide. She studied the swollen pink flesh as she leaned down. "I'm gonna make you scream," she said, her breath hot on Brett's pussy. She ran her tongue up and down Brett's swollen clit, pausing, slowly circling and teasing every inch of wet flesh. She pinched Brett's nipples.

It was like a jolt of electricity connecting Brett's nipples to her clit. She felt ravished and open. She hadn't been fucked in the light for some time, and it was nice to see Allie's blonde head burrowing between her thighs, her hair fanned across her legs. She felt Allie's tongue moving up and down her clit, savoring her. Brett groaned, arching against the cupboard. Allie began to finger Brett.

"Oh, God, put it in." Brett groaned again. The heat radiated throughout her stomach and in the tops of her thighs. Her legs felt weak. Allie shoved three fingers inside her, then pulled them back out while she beat her tongue back and forth over Brett's clit.

Brett's muscles tightened and released, as Allie exposed and explored her naked body, doing what she wanted to with her. Brett bucked and arched as she closed in on orgasm, and still Allie went on, pinching Brett's nipples while her other hand dove relentlessly in and out.

Brett screamed as her body went out of control.

CHAPTER SEVEN

June 15, 1967

I now know that Jen is my soul-mate as much as Elise is. These are the two people that I belong with. Everyone else is extraneous.

Jen just graduated from high school. She wants me to move away from Alma with her. I am tempted, but I know that I may not be able to finish school if I leave now. If I am to be a writer, I still have much to learn. Also, I cannot leave Elise alone with him. Perhaps when Elise and I graduate, we will all move far away from this town, just Elise, Jen and I. I know we can make it. We have our love and our friendship, and we are all capable of much hard work in order to create our own lives.

This all began the day Jen graduated. She took me deep into the park, to the place she first made love to me. She said that she knew what he did to me, that she had it guessed before she ever touched me, but that she knew for certain when she first made love to me.

She is the only one I have ever told what he does to me in the middle of the night, how he touches me, how he says that I belong to him. I was afraid Jen would hate me for it, but I couldn't stop myself, I just poured it all out, and she sat and listened, then held me.

As Brett read this, she was again reminded of Storm, and the way Storm's stepfather had treated the girl who had grown up to be an erotic dancer. Brett's heart went out to Liza, as it had to Storm. She knew the horrors these women had faced, being in an abusive household, with a father or siblings or both who did what they wanted to you because you weren't a real person, you weren't a real human being — you were their possession.

That was when Jen asked me to leave with her. She told me she would love me forever, and that she wanted to save me from that evil man. I told her about school and about Elise, and she said she didn't understand, but she would wait for me until I was ready. She wanted me to know that she would always be there for me.

Elise is dating a new boy, Tom Ringer, and he seems to be very good for her. He is gentle and kind and concerned. I like him a lot. Perhaps he will take care of Elise for me, for, right now, she tells me she'd never be able to live without me. Although Elise and I have grown apart during the past year, we are still both of the same — we each are what the other lacks, and no matter who else enters our lives, I cannot imagine life without Elise.

Brett sat considering this last paragraph. Perhaps it wasn't some strange hippie . . .

Allie came up behind her and put an arm around her. "You're up early," she said, nuzzling Brett's neck.

"Yeah, I couldn't sleep," Brett replied, leaning back in her chair. She was wearing only her flannel bathrobe.

"And I thought I wore you out last night."

Brett smiled, remembering. "You did." She ran her hand down over the opening of Allie's short, red silk bathrobe.

"But you decided Liza was more interesting than cuddling with me this morning, huh?" Allie teased and Brett shrugged, feeling guilty. "Come up with any new clues?"

"Maybe." Brett fingered the page of the last entry. "Listen to this." Allie listened intently as Brett read the entry to her. When she was finished, she leaned back in her chair.

"Are you thinking maybe Elise isn't as innocent as she appears?" Allie asked.

"The question did pop to mind," Brett replied, briefly taking Allie's hand into her own, wondering if she could really understand what all this meant to her.

"Why do I have a feeling nothing's gonna get done to this house till we get to the bottom of this?"

Brett pulled out a notepad and started writing. "Probably because it's the truth," she said with a grin. A few minutes later she handed a sheet to Allie. "Can I get you some coffee?" she asked as Allie began studying the sheet.

WHO	*WHAT*	*WHERE*
The McDonalds	Jen's parents — what do they think?	?
Sylvia Richards	Old co-worker of Carl Swanson	Alma Sun
Gertrude Jarvis	Neighbor quoted in paper	?
Bill & Nancy Taylor	Neighbors	?
Kyle & Judy Spencer	Neighbors	?
Tom Ringer	Elise's boyfriend	Alma
Jeff Brougham	Suspected boyfriend	?
Guy Bradley	Same	?
Michael Stone	Same	?
Elise Swanson(?)	Twin sister	?
Margaret Swanson	Mother	?Colorado
Carl Swanson	Father	?Colorado
Jen McDonald	Accused	Jail
H.V.	Hippie Vagabond	????????

"Where did you get all these names?" Allie asked in amazement when Brett returned with the coffee, having changed into a flannel shirt and jeans.

"Mostly people quoted in articles," Brett said, reexamining the list. "I figure they're our best chances for further information. Maybe someone will give us something we can use."

"I get most of this, but 'suspected boyfriend'?"

"Those are the guys who stepped forward about dating, or having dated, Liza. Perhaps now they'd admit to lying. The major problem is finding everyone."

"I can check the library — between the phone books and the Internet, I may come up with something..." Allie began.

"And I'll check with Sylvia at the *Sun*. Maybe she'll know something. But you should call Tom Ringer — see if he's still in contact with Elise."

The next morning Brett, dressed in black loafers, gray slacks, a shirt, tie and blazer, headed back to the *Alma Sun* to again talk with Sylvia Richards. She and Allie had lost the entire day before to waiting around for furniture to be delivered. Brett had been chomping at the bit to get going on this, but Allie had put her foot down, insisting that they both needed to spend some time on the house.

"The McDonalds?" Sylvia now said to Brett. "Shore I know where they live. Same place they did when they came to town — out by the country club," she said, writing an address down on a piece of paper and handing it to Brett. "It's the ritzier part of town," she added with a frown, fingering the silver cross that hung from her neck. "Should've been them and not the Swansons runnin' from town, but they said they wasn't gonna be run outta town by some loud mouthin' hypocrite. Their words, not mine."

"So they never moved?" Brett asked as she assessed Sylvia more fully. Once again, the seventy-something woman wore pastels: a pink shawl tossed over her powder-blue polyester blouse, a below-the-knee skirt, falling-down stockings and low, bulky, black shoes. The silver cross was her only ornamentation.

"Nope, just dug their heels in, sayin' neither they nor their daughter did nothin' wrong, and if'n they moved, it'd be like they were sayin' she did."

"What about anyone else on this list?" Brett asked, showing her the list she had made that morning with Allie. Sylvia took the list, put on the reading glasses that hung around her neck and glanced at it.

"Well, James Jarvis passed away in, oh, I think it was back in eighty-six, but Gertrude's in a nursing home."

"Which one?"

"It's just over on State Street by Downey."

Brett jotted this in her notebook.

"Bill and Nancy Taylor?" Sylvia continued. "Well, they moved outta town back in the late seventies and I just really don't know whatever became of them, but as for Kyle and Judy Spencer — why, they're still your neighbors."

"Really?"

"Yup, hang a left out your front door, cross the street and you'll be a-sittin' on their front lawn, opposite sides of you as that kooky Madeline Jameson." Sylvia paused briefly to shake her head as if baffled, Brett supposed, by Madeline's differing views. "Now, Jeff Brougham, he's a real sweet boy. Lives with his momma down at the Meadows Trailer Park, and Guy Bradley, last I heard, had himself an apartment just outside a Lansing."

"What about Michael Stone?"

"Died in the Vietnam war, God rest his soul. I didn't care much for all that mess, but he was always a fine young man."

"Hmm . . . You've been most helpful, Mrs. Richards."

"Oh, please, nobody round here calls me that . . ."

"All right, Sylvia," Brett answered. "You've been most helpful, but I was wondering if perhaps you'd have a few moments to answer some questions yourself?"

"Sure, I got lots of time, right now, which is kinda strange, though. Usually during the school year them teachers keep me jumpin'. We have a lot of civic pride here in Alma, you see. The teachers like to make them young'uns study the local history — as recorded in the *Sun*." The woman was all but bursting with pride, Brett noted with distaste. How could anyone ever be so in love with a town?

"Oh, I understand," Brett said, pulling out her tape recorder. She had decided to play her "writer" persona to the max. "Would you mind if I record our conversation?"

"Just so long as you don't ask me nothin' personal," Sylvia replied with a wink. She seemed to be a bit spunkier than Brett was giving her credit for.

"I just mostly want to know what you thought about the Swansons," Brett said, hitting the record button on the machine.

"Why, Carl Swanson was the absolute salt of the earth. I'll have you know, in the fifteen years he worked for John, he was never late or sick a single day."

"Is that so?"

"I was the secretary, I should know. And I also know that you don't see that sort of dedication these days. I know kids who call in sick just because they got an ingrown hair. But Carl, Carl could be runnin' a hundred and ten degree fever, and he'd be in just the same. And when John would tell him to go home, he'd just ignore him and keep right at those cars."

"So he was very conscientious," Brett said, thinking. "I bet he was never even late from lunch," she added, figuring this entire line of questioning to be a dead end. Obviously, Sylvia Richards was president of the Carl Swanson fan club.

"Well, actually, he was late one time. One time in fifteen years. And that was on account of his car breaking down."

"His car broke down?" Brett repeated, enjoying the irony of a mechanic's car breaking down.

"Yup. He went out to run some errands for his wife during lunch — that was the sort of man Carl Swanson was — always thinkin' 'bout and helpin' out his family . . ."

"So his car broke down," Brett said, trying to get Sylvia back on track.

"Blew a gasket, or an oil leak, or somethin' like that. So he fixed it and got right back to work, apologizing for the rest of the day. Course, he didn't let on how bad the car was, but I knew."

"How'd you know?" Brett asked, trying to be polite. She didn't want to spoil Sylvia as a possible contact for other information.

"Well, I looked up at him and said, 'Carl, that's not the uniform you were wearing this morning,' and he said, 'No, Syl.' He always called me Syl. So he says, 'No, Syl. I messed that one up fixin' my car, but I had this one in my trunk.' The man carried a spare uniform in his trunk — talk about dedication!"

Brett managed to escape a few minutes later, ostensibly because she had further interviews, but Sylvia told her to come back anytime, anytime at all.

Over lunch, Brett and Allie compared notes and laid out further game plans. It was decided that Allie would interview Brougham and Bradley, since her more feminine appearance would probably go over better with them, as well as the Spencers, because, she claimed, she didn't want them to get the wrong impression of their new neighbors, which of course Brett would give them.

That left Brett with the McDonalds, Jen, and Gertrude Jarvis. She decided to start in town and leave Jen for tomorrow or the next day, when she had more time.

Martha McDonald answered the door. She was a distinguished-looking woman, probably in her mid-sixties. Her gray hair was tied back in a bun and there was a stern set to her jaw. She wore gray pumps, a light gray skirt and a plain white blouse with a string of what Brett imagined to be real pearls around her neck.

"May I help you?" she asked as she quickly appraised Brett.

"Martha McDonald?" Brett asked, doubtfully. From Liza's diaries, she imagined the McDonalds to be more, well, more hick.

"Yes. And you are . . . ?"

"Bre . . . Samantha Peterson," Brett said, sticking out her hand as she caught herself about to give her old name.

"Well, Bre . . . Samantha, what can I help you with?" Martha asked, looking Brett straight in the eye. Brett got the uneasy feeling she knew Martha from somewhere, and that Martha knew far too much about her. She suddenly felt very young and naive.

"This is really awkward," Brett confessed, nervously running her hand through her short, black hair. "But I'm a writer . . ." She felt off-base. Not only was Martha McDonald not what she expected, but she was also not the sort of people Brett was used to dealing with.

"We don't talk to writers anymore," Martha said sternly, about to shut the door. Brett shoved her hand in the doorway, needing, no, wanting to talk to this woman more. She couldn't quite place it, but it was almost as if some unknown force were compelling her to do this.

"Wait," she begged. "Please, just a few minutes, and I'll convince you to talk with me."

"Very well, then," Martha said, allowing Brett entry. A few moments later, they were arranged in the McDonalds' well-appointed sitting room. Or, that was the way Brett would explain it later to Allie, the only way Brett could think to describe it.

"I'm not really a writer," she confessed. "It just seems that that's the best way to get people to talk about it ..."

"So what are you?"

"An interested party." She went on quickly, before Martha could kick her out, "You see, my lover and I recently moved into the old Swanson place ..."

"I'd heard someone moved in there," Martha said. Brett raised an eyebrow. "This *is* a small town, Ms. Peterson. Word travels fast. At first I thought that was a nice thing, but then I learned otherwise."

"Well, we heard the stories, and the rumors, so we decided to do some research."

"Tell me, is she still there?"

"My lover?"

"No. Liza." There was a pause, and when Brett didn't say anything, Martha said, "There's no doubt in my mind that she's still there. I've always been a rational individual, Ms. Peterson, but there's too much there that defies rational thinking."

"I think she's still there."

"So why did you buy the house — knowing the history and feeling the cold draft?"

"We didn't know the history until after we moved in. As for the cold draft ..." Brett shrugged, searching Martha's eyes, and decided to tell the truth. "I never felt it. When I first entered the house, I felt a warm embrace."

Martha arched her eyebrows at this, then sank back in her chair. "What did you want to ask me?"

"I wanted to ask you what happened," Brett said, tossing aside all of her prepared speeches and questions.

Martha stood, lit a cigarette and walked over to

the window. "We moved here in nineteen-sixty-four. John had been transferred to the Mount Pleasant office, and I decided I wanted to give small-town living a try. Even then there was a rising crime rate in the cities, riots were happening all over, and I decided that life might be better for Jen in a small town. If only I had known then what I know now . . ."

"I think all of us say that at some point in our lives," Brett replied, thinking of her own lost chances.

"Even you?" Martha asked, turning to stare at her.

"Even me." Not only Storm, but her other friends — and now she had to go on, trying to replace the lost shards of her life.

"At what? Thirty?"

"Twenty-eight," Brett admitted, dropping her head.

"Bad affair?" Martha guessed.

"No, someone killed my lover."

Martha nodded in empathy and turned around. "They say Jenny killed hers. Yes, Ms. Peterson, I knew about Jenny and Liza. Jenny told me everything, including how that no-good son-of-a-bitch Carl Swanson treated his daughter." She turned and looked at Brett. "I bet you didn't know that. That the God-fearing town preacher repeatedly raped his daughter from the time she was eight years old."

"I had guessed."

"So tell me how — it's not something that anyone in this town would ever think, let alone say out loud. Or believe," Martha said accusingly.

"I found Liza's diary."

"She kept a diary?" Martha asked, amazed.

"Yes, she did. I haven't finished it yet, and it only begins at the time she met Jen, but . . ."

"Where did you find it?"

"Underneath an old bureau." Brett watched as Martha sat and held her head in her hands. She felt a bit more confident now they were on surer ground. "She never really says it, but the implications are quite clear."

"So you don't think Jenny did it."

"I never did. And neither does Tom Ringer."

"Nice boy. He was one of the few who stood by Jenny's side. Even Liza's sister Elise turned against Jenny in the end. Of course, that was probably her father's doing."

"So who do you think did it?"

"When it happened, I was as shocked as anyone. I fully bought into the 'hippie vagabond' story, but..."

"But what?"

"But in my heart, which I've come to believe more and more as I've grown older, I don't think that was it."

"So who...?"

"Who do you think did it?"

"You're implying it was Carl Swanson?" Brett was surprised.

"I'd like to think it was. But it didn't fit his m.o. you know, keep it quiet, don't let anyone know. But he was so quick to find Jenny's connection as soon as the trail got cold on the stranger... And the hate he spewed forth from his church was unbelievable — especially from a supposedly religious man."

"But he was at work when the murder happened."

"That's the one flaw in the story."

There was a pause. Martha lit a cigarette and Brett quickly did the same. Martha glanced at Brett's lighter and smiled — it was an engraved Zippo, complete with a heart. Storm had given it to her many years before. Brett had a veritable collection of Zippos from old lovers.

"Can I get you anything to drink?" Martha asked, relieving the cold silence.

"Sure," Brett said, carefully pocketing the lighter.

"Myself, I'm in the mood for a scotch."

"That sounds good," Brett replied, glancing at her watch. At least it was past noon. She felt she deserved it and hoped Allie would understand. Allie had pointed out to her how much her drinking had increased during her last years in Detroit, and they both decided it wasn't a good thing.

"Your lover," Martha said, pouring them each a scotch, "is female, correct?"

"Yes," Brett admitted, somewhat nervously. "Her name is Allie."

"John and I were in closing in on forty when we moved here," Martha began, handing Brett a Glenlivet single malt. The woman had taste. "But we tried to be 'hip.' I wanted Jenny to know she could tell me anything." She paused, swirling the liquid around in her glass so the ice clinked against the sides of the glass. "I must admit, however, that it did come as something of a shock when Jenny told me she was in love with Liza, but I decided that in this world, so filled with hate as it is, it's nice to find love."

"Yes, it is," Brett said, thinking of how lucky she was to have found Allie.

"Ms. Peterson . . ."

"Please, call me Sam."

"Well then, you may call me Martha." She paused, slowly smiling. "Sam, I said earlier that I've learned to follow my heart — what I feel, instead of always just what I think."

89

"Yes?"

Martha sat back and stared at her. "Well," she began with difficulty. Seeing Martha's wall down put Brett more at ease. "Well, everyone I've known who has walked into that house since the murder has felt a cold draft, everyone including myself. But you say you didn't."

"I wouldn't lie to you, Mrs. McDonald — Martha." Brett got the uneasy feeling she knew where this conversation was leading.

"I'm not saying you did. What I am saying is that you're the first lesbian to own that house. Perhaps that's why she chose you."

"She chose me?" Brett echoed, again nervously running her hand through her hair.

"I've always felt a presence in that house — and I've never claimed even the smallest psychic power — that's why I believe she is still there."

"But choosing me?"

"With the 'warm embrace,' she chose you. And I'm just trying to figure out why."

"Maybe it's because I'm a lesbian."

"But what did your lover feel?"

"She felt the cold draft," Brett admitted reluctantly. Martha was the first person to whom she had explained the warm embrace, although she and Allie had discussed the draft on many occasions in the three weeks they'd been there.

"Then why you in particular?"

Brett shrugged. She had been wondering the same thing. Martha looked at her, then got up and pulled a photo album off a nearby bookshelf. She handed it to Brett, who eagerly began to flip through its pages. As she studied the pictures she felt she was entering the

90

past in more ways than one. She entered the realm of 1966 and 1967, but as she looked at the snapshots, she became more certain that Liza may have been not only Elise's twin but also Storm's. The pictures took her back to the days when Storm was happy and playful and young, and alive.

Martha watched the expressions on Brett's face. "She reminds you of someone you once knew."

"The lover who was killed."

"You're too young to have had such a tragedy," Martha said, still watching, before a thoughtful expression crossed her face. "If you're twenty-eight, you were born in sixty-seven?"

Brett took a deep breath and said, "I was born on November thirteenth, nineteen-sixty-seven."

"Oh my God." The two women met each others' eyes. Brett nodded and she continued, "Sam, through the years I've leaned a great many things, and one of them is there is no such thing as coincidence."

"I was born at about two-fifteen p.m."

Martha leaned forward, took a sip of her scotch, and looked up at Brett. "Tom and Elise found the body at approximately two-thirty. It was still warm. The police arrived shortly thereafter, and all indications were that, had Tom and Elise shown up even fifteen minutes earlier, they may have stopped it from happening."

Brett barely controlled the shiver that worked its way through her body, starting at her toes. She had tried to ignore the time factor, but now she had to recognize it for what it was, and she wasn't at all pleased with the implications.

Martha continued to look at her, and Brett couldn't even begin to consider the possibilities, so she

91

shrugged and returned to the album. The pictures of Jen and Liza caught Brett's attention. Jen always looked at Liza with love, and as the album's story went on the photos showed Liza returning the feelings. Obviously, the two women had been very much in love and very happy together. These pictures added further fuel to Brett's need to see Jen freed of the charges.

"So how did you manage to pick this godforsaken place?" Martha asked, pulling Brett out of her reverie.

"Allie and I knew we wanted to come back to Michigan, so we grabbed a map, threw a dart at it and it landed on Alma. Then we just fell in love with the house."

"You knew it was your home," Martha said, and Brett nodded. "So where are you from, originally?" Brett didn't answer. Martha sat back and considered her. "You had a map of the entire state of Michigan on the wall, and somehow your dart landed on Alma." It wasn't a question.

Even though she didn't believe in fate, Brett still shivered as she realized what this implied.

CHAPTER EIGHT

"I didn't get out to see Guy Bradley yet," Allie said as she set about fixing the only thing she seemed to know how to cook for dinner, which was burgers, "but Jeff Brougham is sticking to his story."

"Which is?"

"That he was dating Liza just before her murder."

"And what do you think about that?"

"I think it's a load of bullshit. Jeffie is a real momma's boy — I doubt he's ever gotten laid, or ever will."

Brett had gotten home a little after Allie. She

hadn't gotten a chance to speak with Gertrude Jarvis, but she quickly filled Allie in on the details of her interview with Martha McDonald, all the details except about the time of her birth.

"What about the Spencers?"

"They thought the Swansons were ideal neighbors — always there to give a hand with a leaky faucet or a dirty carburetor, or lend a cup of sugar. If Sylvia Richards is the president of Carl Swanson's fan club, then the Spencers are members in good standing." Allie brought the food to the table and they sat down to eat on Brett's old hardwood kitchen table with its comfortable leather chairs.

"Did they notice anything the day of the murder?"

"Nada. Kyle was at work, and Judy was across town, interestingly enough, with Margaret, playing cards."

"And their kids?"

"They were just married then, and they're only about fifty now — so they hadn't even started their brood."

"Lots of dead ends with very few leads."

"How're we ever gonna do this?" Allie asked, shaking her head.

"I don't know." Brett put down her napkin and went into the living room. She poured herself a scotch and stood with her head leaned against the wall. Allie had done a nice job with this room, with the entertainment center and bookshelves nicely accenting the sofa and love seat. The large Oriental rug that took up most of the room brought a bit of color to it all.

"Brett?" Allie asked a few moments later, looking concerned. She lightly laid a hand on Brett's shoulder.

Brett had been thinking of Jen and Liza, which made her think of Storm. "What's going on?" Allie led Brett to the sofa. "What aren't you telling me?"

Brett turned and looked into Allie's deep blue eyes. The woman could read her too well. "The trail of dead bodies . . . It's followed us."

"Oh, baby," Allie said, pulling Brett into her arms. "This one's been gone a long time."

Brett pulled away and looked up at Allie. "But I saw it."

"What?"

"The night before the movers came — you were in Lansing and I was here sick . . ."

"And drinking yourself into oblivion."

"No, I hadn't had anything to drink when the lights went out."

"You didn't tell me that."

"No. I thought it was a Nyquil-induced delusion. I checked the lights, then I came down here to fiddle with the circuit breaker and that's when I saw her."

"Saw who?"

"Liza," Brett said with a gulp. "She was lying right here." She stood to point out the precise location.

"Brett, she's been dead a long time." Allie got up and tried to put her arms around her.

Brett shrugged her away. "I didn't know it was her at the time — I didn't know what it was, but now I know it was her, because I've seen pictures. She was lying there, then she got up, looked at me and said something like 'But who listens when the dead speak?' "

"Then what happened?" Allie asked, sitting down on the couch.

"Then she disappeared, the lights went on and I had a drink."

"So why didn't you tell me?"

"I thought I was imagining things . . . I felt silly."

"What changed your mind?"

"Well, the next day, Tom came here and started telling us those stories . . ." Brett's voice faded and she took another sip of her drink. "Today, when I was talking with Martha, she brought something up, and, well . . ." She paused. Might as well just get it out in the open. "There's a good possibility that I was born at the exact time that Liza Swanson died."

"I had put together the birthday thing, but . . ."

"I was born at two-fifteen, and when Tom and Elise found the body, at two-thirty, it was still warm."

"And she was last seen leaving school with Jen at about eleven . . ." Allie said, letting the implications lie where they would, then she smiled and pulled away. "Oh, Brett."

"It's just plain spooky," Brett grumbled, downing her scotch.

"Ooo, big bad Brett Higgins admits to being scared of something," Allie teased as she wrapped her arms around Brett's neck. Brett glowered at her.

"Back in Detroit," Brett said, her arms around Allie's waist, "I knew what to expect. I knew I'd be shot at, or harassed, or followed. Here, I thought I was safe — and we barely move in before I find a dead body."

"Brett, nobody's gonna be shootin' at you, nobody's goin' to be trying to kill you, or me. We're safe now."

Brett looked at her, then took a step away. She poured herself another scotch, but didn't drink it. Instead, she looked at Allie. "Do you remember

Denise? She was with me the day we first met at the Affirmation's lesbian rap group . . ." Allie nodded and smiled. Denise had set them up. "She and I dated when we were freshmen in college," Brett continued. "And she took me home with her for spring break. This wouldn't've been a big deal, except that her family was very well-to-do. They lived in California."

"She took you across the country to meet her folks?"

"Yup. And it was a big deal to me at the time." Her family had been dirt poor. "It wasn't until I started working for Rick that I had any money of my own." She looked down at her drink, then looked at Allie. "When we were out there, we went to Tahoe for a few days to do some hiking and camping. Anyway, we found Upper Lake Angora, and it was beautiful."

Growing up in the city, she had never had much experience with the country, or beautiful sunsets, or lush mountain lakes, clean air and a view that went on for miles.

"At the end of this lake were two cliffs, one about twenty feet high, and the other about sixty feet. Now, being a mountain lake, this was a really deep lake, and people were diving off the lower cliff. So Denise and I joined in. But that afternoon, I told her I wanted to jump off the higher one." Brett stopped, remembering how Denise had laughed and told her she was nuts. Defiantly, she swam across the lake and climbed to the very top of the other cliff. She caught her breath as she stood looking over the water, then smiled and waved to Denise, who stood at the top of the lower cliff. Brett had been full of bravado and daring.

"So did you?" Allie asked, carefully watching her.

"Well, I stood at the top of the cliff and looked down at the water. Sixty feet seemed a lot higher from that angle . . ." She paused, remembering feeling so alone as she stood by herself at the cliff's peak. "But I ran to the edge and literally tossed myself off."

Allie smiled. "So you did it."

"Yeah, but when I was falling, I looked down expecting to see the water, and instead, I saw the cliff beneath my feet. I realized that the wind had changed, grown stronger, and it was blowing me into the cliff. That was why no one was jumping off the high cliff. And as I was falling, I knew I was going to hit the water as a bloody, crumpled, heaving mass."

"But you didn't."

"No, I didn't — but I thought I was going to. I mean, I knew I was going to die."

"Did your life flash before your eyes?" Allie asked, with a grin.

"No, but I was afraid, and I did wonder what death would be like." She paused again, her heart racing as she remembered how the adrenaline had pumped through her system. "Then my feet were hitting something — but it didn't hurt, as I expected." Not the hard, unyielding surface of the cliff, but rather the soft, pliable surface of the lake, coming up to consume her. As she shot down through the water, unable to stop her momentum, she realized she was alive, and she was grateful.

"Brett?" Allie asked, standing in front of her. Brett looked up into Allie's eyes and smiled.

"When 'Nise told her family about it, they asked me if I'd do it again."

"And what did you say?"

" 'Yeah, why not?' And it was the truth."

"But . . . ?" Allie asked, waiting.

"But I'm not sure if I would now."

"So you're a little older and wiser."

"No, that's not it. It's as if I thought I was invincible — and that's why I was able to do the things I did, to be who I was. But now I'm scared, and I don't know what's going to happen." She ran her fingers down Allie's cheek. "It's like, I've thought back to that night on the roof, and had nightmares that my luck had changed, and somehow the wind that didn't blow me into the cliff has come back to haunt me."

Allie paled and pulled away. Brett pulled her back into her arms.

"Oh, honey, it's not really about that, though," Brett said, hugging her. "It's about the fact that you and Frankie are the only people left that I really care about. And I've just realized this, and I don't know what I'm gonna do about it. I guess I'm scared of being alone."

Allie looked up at Brett. "That I can relate to," she said. "We've both had so much taken from us . . ."

They stood holding each other. Brett thought of all they had lost, and thanked the powers that be that they still had each other. She pulled away a bit to look into Allie's eyes. "I love you," Brett said, meaning it, and enjoying the feel of the words. Three words, three simple words that had taken her so long to say those few years ago.

Allie smiled and kissed her, then took her hand and led her up the stairs to their bedroom. She pulled the blinds shut on the day, which was quickly drifting away to dusk.

Brett ran her fingers over Allie's face, her hair, her

lips, before gently kissing her. Although they both enjoyed fucking, and playing, sometimes their love-making meant more.

She unbuttoned Allie's blouse, then released Allie's breasts from the restraints of her bra. She slowly ran her own lips over Allie's as she cupped Allie's breasts and fingered her nipples. She bowed her head to taste the warm flesh of Allie's breasts, to tease Allie with her tongue. Her teeth played over Allie's increasingly tense and swollen nipples as the little buds burst forth for further attention.

Allie helped Brett undress and when they were both naked, standing inches from each other, Brett lifted Allie and carried her to the bed, where she laid her tenderly on the covers.

Allie moaned when Brett climbed on top of her, spreading Allie's legs apart. The beauty of Allie's naked body always took Brett's breath away: the soft, gentle curves, the blond hair nestled between her legs, the tender skin, the way Allie would wrap her long legs around Brett's back or neck. She toyed with Allie's breasts and nipples, ran her tongue down from Allie's neck to her belly button.

Allie reached up to grab the headboard as Brett spread her legs further apart. Brett knew she liked the feeling of giving all power and control to her, liked being spread out for her and letting her do whatever she wanted. Brett knew she longed for slow, careful ministrations to every part of her body — breasts, stomach and inner thighs — and that she enjoyed the feel of Brett's lips, fingers and tongue touching her everywhere. She wanted Brett to take her.

Brett climbed between her legs, spreading her lips wide, blowing on the moist flesh. The mild sensation drove Allie wild, and she arched, begging to be taken. Brett inserted first one, then two fingers, impaling her, and after she came, Brett crawled on top of her and said, "I love you."

Later that night, as they lay in bed naked, watching TV and drinking almond-and-cinnamon-flavored milk with whipped cream, Brett looked at Allie, who lay in her arms.

"Y'know, I think I'd be upset if you ever called me Sam when you came," she said, referring to her assumed name.

Allie rolled over and looked at her. "I first fell in love with Brett Higgins, and it'd be tough changing something like that."

That night, Brett dreamed she was in the bedroom making love to Allie, just as they were a few hours before . . .

But then she realized she was really making love to Storm, except then Jen entered and watched them. And Brett looked down and realized she was really making love to Liza . . .

Then she heard her father yell her name: "Brett!" And she jumped up and was clothed and running down a hallway, and she knew she had been there before. She kept running, trying to close him out as she pushed through door after door. He was chasing her, and then she fell and he was upon her, but she rolled away and looked up at him.

It wasn't her father. She had never seen this man before in her life.

She awoke with a start, grateful that she hadn't awakened Allie, who slept like a log. She pulled on a robe and padded downstairs to her study, where she sat on the leather love seat, looking up at the pictures Allie had, thankfully, allowed her to mount on the wall. Allie had pictures of her own family throughout the house, but these were the only photos Brett wanted.

There were three pictures: One was Rick DeSilva, her old boss, who had been like a father to Brett, sitting with his feet up on his oak desk, talking on the phone and grinning at the camera. The second was Storm on Christmas day, opening a gift Brett had given her. The third picture was of Rick, Storm, Frankie and her, standing in the box office of the Paradise Theater, grinning at the photographer.

The only two people in this last picture who were still alive were Frankie and Brett. She brushed the thought aside and pulled Liza's diary out from the antique rolltop desk. She was almost finished with it.

November 12, 1967

I'm not sure if school is worth it. Everything would be so much easier if I were to run away with Jen.

Carl has accused me of unnatural behavior with Jen. I told him that whatever I do comes as naturally to me as what he does with me. That got me hit. But the pain from that wasn't as bad as the pain from thinking of life without Jen. He went on about the

*wrath of God, and all of that, but then he told me that
I "belonged to him."*

*Sometimes I wish I were dead, thinking that maybe
then he'd realize how horrible he'd been to me for all
those years. Thinking that maybe then my mother
would realize she might've been able to do something.*

The page here was smudged, so Brett carefully
examined it before realizing that Liza had probably
been crying when she wrote it. She could even picture
beautiful Liza writing, hurriedly, her words spilling out
of her as the tears poured down her face and onto the
paper, and she angrily wiped the page.

*My father goes into church every Sunday and
preaches of a God I do not know. His God is angry
and vengeful, yet I look at the trees and sky and river
and into Jen's eyes, and I know that whoever created
this couldn't be the same God Carl yells at me about.*

The rest of the page was blank. Brett quickly
flipped the page, wanting more, but worried that this
was the end.

November 13, 1967
*I can't sleep. Terrible nightmares. I know there's
nothing wrong with me, but some part of me is afraid
that Carl is right, that I'm the spawn of the devil.*

*Now, with the light on, I know he's wrong, but I
can't help but worry.*

*And now Jen's told me that her mother knows
about us, and part of me thinks it's so unfair that her*

parents can accept us like this, but another part is thankful, because, maybe with them, we could actually make it on our own.

All I really know is that something has to happen. I'm afraid all the time and can't sleep at night unless I'm with Jen. Otherwise, I just want to curl up and die.

The entire journal had been written in nearly perfect cursive writing, with a blue pen. Now Brett saw words, literally scrawled across the page, in red pen:

Do you listen when the dead speak?

She suddenly felt someone watching her. She bolted to her feet and stared at the empty room. "And what if I do?" she said aloud.

CHAPTER NINE

"What you have to realize, Brett dear, is that the dead are always speaking to us — in all sorts of different ways, by all sorts of different methods." Madeline sat back in her chair and sipped her coffee. "The dead never truly leave us."

"Not all of us communicate with spirits, Madeline," Brett grumbled as she stared out the window.

Madeline didn't have a class till later that day and had decided to pay Brett and Allie a visit. First thing that morning, Allie had commented on Brett's restless night, so Brett told her about the journal entry, deciding that Allie may as well join her in the full lunacy of the moment, and of course Allie felt a need to tell Madeline. The three were in the kitchen, discussing the life, and death, of Liza Swanson.

"Allison," Madeline said, looking at Allie. "Both of your parents are dead, correct?"

"Yes," Allie said, shaking her head.

"But they continue to affect you in profound ways. They live on with you in spirit. You remember the way they did things, the things they said. And little parts of their physical being live on through you, and will continue to your children, and your children's children."

"But they still don't write her letters in the middle of the night!" Brett was violently disturbed by the fact that when she had pulled out the journal to show Allie and Madeline, the last scrawls had vanished.

"But the dead speak to us through their effects on us, and on others. Even you," Madeline said, ignoring Brett's remarks, "although you keep most of your past a mystery. I do know that you, too, have experienced deaths that have affected you in ways you might not yet realize."

You don't know the half of it, Brett thought.

"The people whose pictures hang in the study, for instance," Madeline said. Brett had forgotten that Madeline had seen the photos. She still was not accustomed to Madeline's scrutiny; nothing made it past the woman's eyes or ears.

"You got me there," Brett admitted. "Two of them are dead."

Madeline nodded sagely. "They affected you and

will continue to affect you for the rest of your life." She paused and carefully searched Brett's eyes. "Both of you have experienced profound loss — death — at a very early age, which intensifies the situation."

"So you're saying that's why Liza picked us?" Allie asked.

Brett looked out the window, thinking they still needed to clean the garage. She wondered what they'd do with the large yard once summer arrived. She had never had much of a green thumb, so maybe she could talk Allie into doing that crazy little thing known as "landscaping" if she were to offer to keep the grass cut and edged.

Her thoughts dribbled across Storm and Rick. Her early retirement from crime had seemed far too simple and easy. There had to be a price for the dead bodies she had left behind. She was starting to understand that they were only just beginning to pay that price. She wondered what the final toll would be.

"Perhaps," Madeline said thoughtfully, interrupting her thoughts. Brett had to think a moment to realize they were discussing why Liza picked them.

"Well," Brett said, with a chuckle, "that and . . . that she died and I was born at the same time."

"Really?" Madeline said.

"We don't know that it was the exact same time," Allie said. "But all things considered, we figure the two events occurred within an hour."

"That is very interesting," Madeline said, leaning back against the table. One could almost see the wheels churning in her head.

"This is all well and good," Brett said. "But this hopeless hypothesis is getting us nowhere."

"Or so it seems at the moment. But if we understand Liza's motives in the situation . . ."

"We might be able to figure out what she wants us to do!" Allie concluded triumphantly.

"We don't know diddly-shit right now," Brett mumbled. She was in a contrary mood this morning.

"We know there's a ghost," Allie interjected.

"And she wants something," Madeline said, ignoring Brett's glare.

"How do we know that? For all we know she's just bored!" Brett said vehemently, hating even to have to admit she might believe in ghosts.

"That wouldn't be rational," Madeline said.

"Oh, and ghosts leaving vanishing messages and playing dead in my living room are rational subjects."

"We know there's a ghost . . ." Allie began.

"She was murdered," Allie continued, "and her lover is in jail for the crime."

"But the evidence was circumstantial at best," Brett added, liking the conversation more now that it was concerned with things of the material level. Her rational mind preferred games with rules, and it didn't appear that there were any rules when dealing with the dead.

"And homophobia played a crucial role in the trial." Allie grimaced.

"To bottom-line it," Brett said, "we really don't have a motive, except with the hippie . . ."

"So our only basic assumption is that the wrong person is in jail for the crime," Allie said.

"But if we're back to the hippie, then we still have one main question," Brett complained. "How does she expect us to find this guy thirty years later? I mean, all we've got to go on are some old sketches from the newspapers."

"Maybe we could get the real sketches from old police files?" Allie asked.

"You haven't checked with the police?" Madeline frowned.

"Lansing mostly handled it because Alma only had one constable at the time," Brett said.

Allie grabbed their interview list from the shelf. "Why isn't his name on here?"

"Because I didn't think about it," Brett replied.

"Just because he's a cop doesn't mean he's a bad person," Allie retorted. Madeline's ears pricked up on this. She clearly hadn't realized that Brett had any problems with the police.

"I just didn't think about it," Brett defended herself.

Allie grabbed a pen. "What was his name?"

"George McFarley."

Allie added the name to the list. "We might as well stay organized about this," she said. "We should finish yesterday's work — you can go talk with Gertrude Jarvis and I'll tackle Guy Bradley, then we can go talk to George McFarley together."

"If we can find him," Brett said.

"And," Madeline said, "if you two don't mind, I'd like to stay here and read Liza's journal. There may be something in it that you missed."

"I think that's a very good idea," Allie said as she went to take a shower.

* * * * *

"Please, call me Trudi," Gertrude Jarvis said a few

hours later as Brett sat in her room at the nursing home. Trudi wore a robe with pajamas underneath and outrageous dinosaur slippers that roared when she walked. "No one but my husband ever called me Gertrude."

"Your husband..." Brett said, nervously.

"Kicked the bucket coupla years ago." Trudi sat down on her bed as a tear slipped down her cheek. "Don't get me wrong — I loved the old fart dearly, but you gotta go on." She paused briefly, glancing at a picture at her bedside. "First chance that asshole son-in-law of mine got, he shoved me in this place."

"I'm sorry..." Brett said, once more not knowing what to say.

"My daughter, she never woulda done this — but, as they say, she fell into the wrong group of people. Kinda like Maggie Swanson."

"What do you mean by that?" Brett asked. Brett had used her writer story and Trudi had made it perfectly clear that she was glad for any company. Brett understood why when she began to see the general condition of the home's inhabitants. Trudi, with her spry eightyish body, did not belong here.

"You said you want to hear about the Swansons, so I'm tellin' you 'bout the Swansons. You see, James and I lived next to them the entire time they were in Alma — but I had known Maggie for a long time before then. I used to babysit her when she was little. Maggie May O'Dell was her name, up until Carl Swanson came to town and swept her off her feet. I never did like that man, and I knew why when they moved next door to us."

"Why?" Brett asked, wondering what Trudi had noticed.

"Well, lemme give you some background-type info. You see, James was from England, and I wouldn't give him the frickin' time of day with his hot shit accent and education and all. We were like fire and ice. But he finally won my heart, and we had Linda. But then we couldn't have any more kids — and I was always thankful James didn't hold it against me. Those days, things were a lot different than they are today, let me tell you."

"I can only imagine."

"So, anyway, James had himself a good job workin' at a desk in Lansing and, with only Linda, I had lots of time on my hands — especially when she started school. So I guess I got the reputation of bein' the neighborhood busybody. You see, I never did get much into TV or reading. I prefer to see life first-hand. James and I used to go all over, once Linda got married and moved out. We been to Europe, and China, and all over this here country of ours." She leaned back and stared at the picture on the table. She reached to the table and grabbed a pack of chewing gum and shoved a piece in her mouth. She offered one to Brett.

"No thanks."

"Doc made me quit smokin' a buncha years back," Trudi said sorrowfully. "I've never quite gotten over that. I shoulda told him to go screw himself — that way, maybe I coulda died with James."

"I've been trying to quit . . ."

"You're young, you still got a long time to live."

"Unless I get hit by a car, fall off a roof, get caught in a gang war . . ."

"Anyway," Trudi began, grinning at Brett. "I always liked to pay attention to what was happenin' around me — and let me tell you, it was better'n any of these soap operas they got on TV today, even in a small town like Alma."

"About the Swansons?" Brett said, refocusing Trudi.

"I knew damn well that man was beatin' on Maggie from the day they moved in."

"Did you say anything to anyone?"

"Honey, we're talkin' the nineteen-fifties and the town preacher. Like anybody'd believe a word I said."

"So how long did this go on?"

"The entire time they lived there. Let me tell you, there was always yellin' and screamin' and bangin' about goin' on in that house. Now, I've never been a regular church-goin' lady — hell, I don't think anybody'd even call me a lady — but even then I knew that was no way for a preacher to be actin'."

"What about Liza and Elise?"

"They were day and night. Liza was always running around, gettin' into trouble, comin' home all scraped up — you could tell the girl just loved life. Elise, on the other hand, she was quiet, withdrawn. She liked to read, but she was always with Liza, and it was like Liza was tryin' to live for the two of them."

"Was there ever any indication that Carl had switched his ... attentions ... to Liza?"

"What makes you ask that?" Trudi said with a start.

"Ah, just little things I've read and heard."

Trudi got up and looked out the window, her dinosaurs roaring all the way. "She was just a little shit, still a girl ... No more'n maybe ten. And I just got this feelin' . . ." She turned and faced Brett. "I couldn't prove anything, or really say anything to anybody because, again, they wouldn't've believed me."

"But?" Brett prodded.

"Well, I noticed Mags wasn't as banged-about-lookin' as before — and by the time Liza got murdered, all that was just about gone. But you see, Liza was lookin' a little banged. Now, she had always been a wild kid, always gettin' into stuff, so she just kept on lookin' like she was still gettin' into trouble. And they were sayin' how she was accident-prone and all, y'know, fallin' offa ladders, runnin' into doors, all very believable if you knew the kinda kid Liza had been."

"But you didn't believe it."

"No, I didn't. You see, kids outgrow that sorta shit by the time they're fifteen, sixteen. Only, Liza didn't. If you believed them."

"Was there anything else?" Brett asked hopefully. This was the first true outsider who had corroborated her facts.

Trudi started to shake her head, then stopped herself. "Along about the same time I thought Carl had decided to start bangin' on her 'stead of Mags, Liza — well, it was as if something in Liza had already gotten up and died, if you know what I mean."

Brett nodded. She remembered that same look in Storm's eyes.

"I'm not exactly sure I know what went on in that house, and I don't think I want to."

Brett nodded again, as she jotted a few more notes in her book. She looked up at Trudi, who suddenly looked very old as she walked over to sit on her bed, the slippers still roaring.

"The day of the murder . . ." Brett said, trying to hide her smirk about the slippers. They looked almost like a stuffed-animal rendition of Puff the Magic Dragon.

"I was across town with Mags playing cards. We had this really big card club, and just about all the women in town who didn't work got together once a month to play cards all day long. It gave us a chance to catch up on the gossip from across town. She was there the entire time, from nine that morning till Carl came with the news at about four."

"You've been through this before." Brett grinned.

"Hell, yes. First old George McFarley, then all those cops from Lansing. All of them askin' exactly the same questions — as if they just couldn't talk to one another. It was me who first told them about that hippie."

"Really? What was the story with that?"

"Well, just about everybody noticed him in town at one time or another during the days before Liza's death, but it was me who had seen him around the Swanson place. Course, the Swansons said they'd never seen him, but I know for a fact that Carl Swanson spoke to him on more than one occasion."

"You saw them speaking?" Brett queried, her ears pricking up. Could there be a connection?

"Hell, yes! And he up and denied it, and the cops believed him because he was a man of God." She said these last words with a facetious tone and bow. "Man of God my ass."

"That's very interesting," Brett said, nodding as she tried to figure how this new information fit into the puzzle. "Is there anything else you can think of that might help me get a more complete picture of the Swansons or the murder?"

"You might want to talk to George McFarley. Last I heard, he was around Detroit. I don't think he ever told anybody what he really thought about it all."

"What makes you say that?"

"I knew George pretty well, and he was a very even-tempered sort of fellow. Well, after the trial, he just seemed to get really pissed, and that's when he up and moved down near Detroit."

"With no hint as to why?"

"Not a word."

"From everything you've said," Brett said as she collected her things, concluding the interview, "I take it you were not displeased when the Swansons moved?"

Trudi grimaced. "Actually, I was real pissed. I mean, I was glad to see that son-of-a-bitch leave town, but I was worried about Maggie and Elise. Elise had closed herself off even more after the death — some said she lost the best part of herself with Liza. But what really got my goat was Swanson's little going-away gift."

"What?"

"You haven't heard about that? Well, it seems he was having car trouble, which I thought was funnier than shit, him bein' a mechanic and all, but everybody in town decided to pitch together to get him a new car. Kinda like makin' up for all those years he was preachin' and not gettin' paid for it."

"And this pissed you off?"

"Hell, yes. I mean, number one: when he was the preacher, all the women kept makin' him food and

115

goodies to make up for his not gettin' paid — and I'm sure all that was worth a pretty penny. Number two: what business do those who ain't got shit have with givin' away what little they got?"

As Trudi fumed, Brett thought, no way, it couldn't be — something this big couldn't have been overlooked. She tried rationalizing it but decided that no matter how slim the chances, it required further investigation.

"Let me ask you this," Brett said, chewing her pencil. "Do you think they got the right person?"

"I can't say. Honey, you have to realize all that took place in a different world. Back then, I thought a fag was a cigarette — James taught me that, him being English and all. I mean, I didn't know squat about gays and lesbians and all that. Nobody did, really. We just thought they were all a bunch of really bad, perverted people."

"You used the past tense. Does that mean you've changed your mind?"

"Honey, after livin' next door to that preacher for so long, and knowin' what he was really like . . . I'm real pissed that people thought so highly of him. After all that, I figure what does a lot of this shit mean just so long as you ain't hurtin' nobody doin' it?"

Brett nodded. She liked this woman. "One last question."

"Shoot," Trudi said.

"Where did you get those slippers?"

Trudi got a big shit-ass grin on her face and stuck her feet out and away from the bed. "You like 'em? My granddaughter gave 'em to me for Christmas." She jumped off the bed and made them roar. "They make me feel like a little kid again!" she exclaimed with a laugh.

Her happiness with something so little was totally infectious.

CHAPTER TEN

"Guy Bradley cracked when I visited him at his apartment in Lansing," Allie said as Brett walked in the front door. "He said he never slept with Liza, nor did Michael Stone, and he doubts that Jeff Brougham had anything to do with her except in his wet dreams."

"Guy told you all that?" Brett said, excited.

"He was a regular font of information. Turns out, he's a flaming fag. He and Michael were lovers during school, and they concocted the story to cover their queerness. Figured they couldn't hurt anybody with it, because Liza was dead."

"Asshole," Brett said, thinking about all the havoc their "harmless" little story had helped to wreak.

"Yeah, it took him a while to realize exactly what they'd done, but then they figured it was too late. Plus they were little chickenshits."

"So what about Jeff?"

"Jeff was always a momma's boy, Guy said, and that as far as he knew had never gotten laid a day in his life. For chrissakes, the boy still lives with his mother."

"I just can't fuckin' believe they turned on Jen and Liza like that," Brett yelled as she pounded the wall, her impatience with all the lies and things unsaid percolating over.

"Brett, honey," Allie said, trying to comfort her. "They were young and scared, and it was a pre-Stonewall world. People just didn't talk about things like we do."

"I know, I know," Brett said, leaning against the wall. "Trudi said the same thing to me."

"Trudi?"

"Gertrude Jarvis."

"What else did she have to say?"

"Quite a bit, in fact. She verified the abuse and molestation, as much as she could — without any prompting from me. She added that Carl had been beating Margaret the entire time they were married — until he switched to Liza, that is."

"But we already knew he beat Liza."

"Yes, but it's nice to have someone on the outside say the same thing."

119

"Did she say anything else?"

"Well, there's one thing that I want to check out before I present it as fact . . ."

"Oh, c'mon, what is it?" Allie urged Brett.

"You can wait," Brett said with a grin, as she dodged Allie, who was ready to tickle the information out of her. She didn't want to get Allie's hopes up on what was, at the moment, mere speculation. She looked around. "Where's Madeline?"

"Oh, she left a note saying she had to leave but would be back later to finish reading the journal. I was reading it, in fact, when you walked in."

"Well, good, keep reading. I have to talk with Sylvia Richards."

"What are you on to?"

"Not telling. You can call your old friend Tom Ringer and see if you can find out just where in Colorado the Swansons moved to, and where Elise is living. Then call information and see if you can find the constable, George McFarley, I think he may be somewhere around Detroit." Brett filled a Thermos cup with diet cola and kissed Allie on the cheek. "I'll be back in a while," she said.

Allie glared at her, obviously not liking her secrecy. They needed more information. Brett had decided she wouldn't raise Allie's hopes with red herrings, but she was also a little superstitious. She worried that if she talked too much about what she was hoping for, it might not come true.

She hoped Allie could locate the Swansons and George McFarley. She wanted to talk with George and Elise before confronting Carl and his wife. She wanted as much of the story as possible, so she wouldn't slip up when talking with him.

She knew without a doubt now that they were in this to the finish, and she knew that that finish had to include talking with Carl Swanson, no matter how badly she wanted to cut him like she did a cigar.

When she pulled into the lot of the *Alma Sun*, Sylvia was just climbing into her car.

"Wait!" Brett yelled, as she threw her black Explorer into park and jumped out. She didn't want to wait until tomorrow to find out.

"You caught me sneakin' out early," Sylvia confessed, standing by her car. Her coat was an old down one that came down over her hips. Somewhere in the back of her mind, Brett remembered how big down had been in the 70's.

"I just have a few quick questions. Could you possibly hold off for just a couple of minutes?"

"What is it you need, dear?"

"I was just talking with Gertrude Jarvis, and she told me the town bought Carl Swanson a car as a going-away present."

"Why, yes, we did. He was such a kind, giving man, it was the least we could do for him, to make his time of trouble a little more bearable. Everybody, and I do mean everybody, even Trudi and James, chipped in to buy him that car. People were scrapin' the bottoms of their piggy banks to make sure we got him a fine automobile."

"Yesterday you told me about his car breaking down . . ."

"That's what made it such a fine gift. It was me who suggested it, you know."

"Well, I was wondering, do you happen to remember what day it was when his car broke down?"

"It was Wednesday, I remember that 'cause Wednesdays were always a real busy day at the shop, and that made it especially tough since Carl took a long lunch that day."

"Do you know the date?" Brett urged.

"Oh," Sylvia said, leaning back against her car and considering the question. "I don't think even John would've kept the records that long . . ."

Brett sighed. No. No one would've kept time cards for thirty years, not even a truly anal-retentive person.

"Wait!" Sylvia suddenly exclaimed. "Oh, dear, this is dreadful." She clasped her hand to her mouth.

"What?" Brett asked, jumping back to life.

"I remember exactly what I thought when I heard about Liza . . ." Sylvia said, trailing off.

"What did you think?" Brett asked eagerly.

"I thought — well, you must promise to never repeat this — it's just too awful . . ."

"I promise," Brett said quickly.

"I thought . . . I thought, 'What an awful day. To have your car break down and have your daughter murdered!' Obviously, the two cannot compare, but that's honest-to-goodness what I thought when I heard about Liza."

Carl Swanson took a long lunch the day his daughter was murdered. Brett almost jumped for joy as one piece fell into place. She couldn't believe the cops hadn't checked into it, but, after all, they *were* cops and Brett never had much respect for the intelligence or honesty of any of their lot.

"Can I ask how this fits in?" Sylvia asked innocently.

122

Brett had to remind herself of what she had told Sylvia her intentions were. "I'm just trying to create the fullest picture I can. Although the two events obviously do not carry the same weight or significance, they were two bad things that occurred in the same time period," Brett said, quickly trying to decide her next words. "That they occurred on the same day is relevant in that his friends and neighbors felt impotent against the terrible crime that had been committed against one of their own, so they attempted to fix the other problem, against which they could do some good."

"I had never thought of it that way," Sylvia replied, fully buying into Brett's bullshit.

"We have opportunity!" Brett yelled as she rushed into the house.

"What?" Allie asked, as Brett grabbed her and danced her around the room.

"We have opportunity — Carl did have the ability to commit the crime."

"We're celebrating because Liza's father could have killed her?"

"Well, okay, you have a point there," Brett said, quickly sobering up and sitting down. She had felt drunk with the excitement of the moment.

"Now, can you slow down and explain?"

"Okay, the only day Carl was ever late to work, or from lunch, was the day of Liza's death. In fifteen years, he was never late and he never called in sick, except that one day when he was late from lunch. Sylvia bragged to me about his punctuality, and mentioned that the one day he was ever late was because his car broke down. Today, Trudi told me his car broke down about the time of Liza's murder. So I went back and asked Sylvia exactly what day it was."

"And she told you it was the same day," Allie concluded. "How come this was never mentioned before?"

"He was the town preacher. He was never even suspect," Brett said, still wondering why the police hadn't checked his alibi.

"Give me all the details," Allie said, her old law enforcement mind taking over.

"Okay, on that day, Carl Swanson left work at lunch supposedly to run a few errands for his wife. He returned late, saying he'd had car trouble. When he returned to work, he was wearing a clean uniform."

"So he had changed out of the bloody one?"

"Precisely. Or that's the assumption I'm running under now. But I would love to find that bloody uniform, or at least figure out what happened to it."

As it turned out, Tom Ringer had also been most helpful. He had kept in some contact with Elise and volunteered not only the Swansons' Colorado address but also Elise's current address. As soon as she had turned eighteen, Elise married and moved back to Michigan, to Bloomfield Hills, with her new husband. It had been a small wedding, and Tom had not even been invited.

George McFarley, however, died in an accident in the early 90's. His widow, still living in Ferndale, Michigan, was more than eager to help in any way she could. Allie told her she'd get back to her if necessary.

"What are you thinking?" Allie asked.

Brett grinned and looked at her. "About a woman with slippers that roar," she said, still smiling.

"What?" Allie asked, grinning herself now.

"Trudi Jarvis," Brett explained. "Her granddaughter gave her these dinosaur slippers that roar when she walks."

"And she actually wears them?"

"Yes," Brett replied, giggling. "And she gets the biggest kick out of them. Says they make her feel like a kid again. I mean, Allie, the woman's eighty if she's a day!"

"Maybe she knows something that we don't — think about it, Brett. How often do we stop to enjoy the little things in life?"

Brett suddenly grew somber and looked at the floor, holding her head in her hands. She looked up at Allie. "Does the pain ever go away?"

Allie leaned forward to take her lover in her arms. "Oh, Brett, I wish I could say it does, but all I know is that it seems to die down until it's a dull ache that you only feel occasionally."

"I know, I know," Brett replied. "I'm supposed to go on to be thankful for the time they gave me, and all that other horseshit."

"Brett," Allie said, pulling back to look at her. "I know you feel lost, because you've been fighting your whole life. But you can't do anything to bring them back, and you can't go on hating Storm's murderer, and your father, and your brothers for your entire life."

"You know?" Brett asked. She had never really filled Allie in on her youth.

Allie nodded. "That you have been able to move on

is one of the reasons I love you like I do. But I do know that some day we'll be able to bring you past it."

That night, Brett slept soundly, surprisingly enough. The day's excitement had worn her thin.

"You know about loss." The voice pulled Brett out of a dead sleep.

"Huh?" she said, looking about for the speaker. Allie grumbled and rolled over. It wasn't Allie's voice. She got up and put on her robe. She wandered to the window to look out at the stars and noticed someone standing by the garage smoking a cigarette.

Brett grabbed her loafers and gun, quickly checking the rounds and chambering it as she ran down the stairs. She bolted out the front door, as quietly as she could bolt, and edged around the house. The figure, unrecognizable in the shadows, entered the garage. Hadn't she locked the side door?

Brett swiftly made her way across the yard, keeping her gun up in check. She approached the open side door to the garage, carefully listening for any voices. She heard none. She had been resting on the assumption that anyone who might want Brett Higgins dead thought Brett Higgins was already dead. Perhaps that had not been a brilliant line of reasoning on her part. Her mind was alert, her eyes wide open, every particle of her being prepared to do battle as she entered the garage.

The figure stood by the old workbench, smoking

the cigarette and watching her. Brett aimed the gun at the figure, but before she had a chance to speak, the figure dropped the cigarette and vanished.

Brett stood, staring at the empty space for a full minute before she flipped on the overhead light. She inspected every inch of the garage — the door was open — did Allie leave it unlocked? She inspected the lock, checking to make sure it was still fully functional: it was. She turned off the light and locked the door behind her. Then she turned around and tried it again, to make sure it was secure.

She went through the house, double-checking that all the doors and windows were locked and that everything was where it should be. She wrote herself a note to call Frankie in the morning, to ensure everyone knew Brett Higgins was dead.

Then and only then did she turn off all the lights and sit on the sofa. She lit a cigarette and stared around the darkened room. Those few adrenaline-filled minutes had made her realize she might never be truly safe. Although some of her old enemies were now dead, there were also some who were still alive, and though they might not care about her anymore, now that she was out of the business, they might care about what she knew and could say.

"Brett?" Storm said lightly.

Brett jumped, startled. Storm was sitting next to her on the couch. This time Brett was sure it was Storm, not Liza. She wore what was always one of Brett's favorite outfits: a light pink silk blouse tucked into a soft pair of black slacks with loafers and trouser socks. Little diamond earrings and a gold and diamond heart necklace, which lay softly on the skin of her upper chest, completed the outfit. Brett had given her that necklace their last Christmas together.

Brett reached over and ran her fingers through Storm's dark, silky tresses. Storm took Brett's hand and held it against her cheek, which was surprisingly warm.

"I never told you how much I loved you," Brett said, her voice deep with regret. A part of her wanted to jump up and tell herself she was just dreaming, but another part took over and let her enjoy these few moments, which she knew were a gift from beyond.

"I knew," Storm murmured softly.

"And then Allie . . ." Brett began, wanting to explain, wanting to ease her conscience, wanting to make it all better.

"Don't," Storm said, laying a finger against Brett's lips. "Don't tell me you wouldn't do it again, because neither of us will ever know that." Brett had simultaneously dated both Storm and Allie. Allie hadn't discovered this until after Storm's death, even though Storm had known all along. "What's important is the time we had together," Storm whispered into her ear, her breath warm against Brett's cheek.

"I loved you so much, and I miss you so much," Brett murmured as she took Storm into her arms, memories of their time together, of how they made love, attacking her mind like the Allied forces at Normandy.

"You can be happy with Allie, if you'll let yourself be," Storm said sadly.

"But . . ." Brett wanted to keep Storm here, with her.

"And maybe, in helping someone else finish their

business, you'll finish some of yours." Storm gently touched Brett's face and hair, as if to memorize her.

"But I don't want to forget you."

"You don't need to. You just have to let me go." Storm pulled back and kissed Brett gently on the lips. "Until we meet again."

CHAPTER ELEVEN

They drove in silence. Brett didn't want to talk about her vision of the night before, and Allie knew better than to pressure her about why she had slept on the couch with a picture of Storm.

They got to the prison right at the start of visiting hours. Jennifer McDonald was surprised to have visitors so early. Her mother usually came later in the afternoon. In almost thirty years, Martha McDonald had never missed a single visitors' day.

"Mom told me about you," Jen said as they picked

up the phones through which they were to communicate. She still looked a bit like the seventeen-year-old they had seen in the pictures, but the years had taken their toll. Her hair was now cut short and streaked with gray, a myriad of wrinkles now graced her face and she had gained a few pounds, but Brett could still see the old Jen underneath if all. In person, though, there was no doubt about it: Jen McDonald was one big bulldyke.

"I don't know what I can add to what she said . . ." Jen said, apparently wishing she could be helpful.

"Did you notice anything that day? As you climbed out the window?" Brett asked.

"No. I just took off. I mean, we figured it was Elise, but Carl did sometimes stop home during lunch . . ."

"And you didn't want him to catch you," Brett finished for her.

"Yuppers. So I just took off running. I didn't even stop to see if there were any cars around," Jen admitted with a shrug. Brett figured she had been through this entire interrogative routine more times than she cared to remember. She bet Jen had cursed her lack of observation more times than a jail guard rattled her keys in a day. She couldn't imagine what it would be like to have the grief of a trial and conviction tossed on top of the loss of a lover. More than once she had wondered why the cops hadn't come after her for Storm's murder, but she chalked it up to a rare bit of good luck that could change if examined too closely.

"Did you have any indication of whether or not

Carl knew about you and Liza?" Brett asked, wondering if Liza had told Jen about Carl's homophobic accusations.

Jen grimaced at this. "Yeah, the night before she died Carl accused her of 'unnatural behavior' with me. Told her I wasn't the sort of person he approved of her hangin' out with."

"What did she say to that?"

"I'm not really sure. We only discussed it briefly." Jen turned away from them. "We thought we had all the time in the world."

"I know how that goes."

"Yeah, Mom mentioned that, but you also have your freedom and a very good-looking woman sitting next to you." She gave Allie a grin as they eyed her.

"What'd she say?" Allie asked Brett.

Brett put her hand over the phone. "She was just complimenting your good looks."

Allie blushed. "Tell her thanks."

"She said thanks." Brett met Jen's grin with one of her own.

"I was seventeen when I was thrown in here. I'm forty-six now. I've spent over half my life behind bars for a crime I didn't commit."

"I wish there were something we could do . . ." Brett said, trying once again to imagine a life behind bars.

"Yeah, I know. My lawyer said the same thing." Jen had the look of a woman who had given up all hope.

"Did you happen to notice any strangers near the Swansons' prior to Liza's murder?" Brett asked suddenly.

"The hippie vagabond routine," Jen replied,

nodding. "Strangely enough, I did. Well, actually, it was Liza who told me she saw Carl talking to some strange-looking long-haired fellow. We just assumed it was someone else he was trying to talk into joining his flock. I think he had half the fucking town brainwashed by the time he was through."

"So I hear." There was a brief pause while Brett tried to remember any other things she had wanted to ask Jen. "During everything Carl did, didn't Liza's mother even try to do anything?"

"No. Never. Liza always dreamed she would, but she didn't." She looked away as a tear crawled from her eye. "Other teenagers dream of becoming movie stars, or singers. Not my Liza, no, she just wanted her mother to do fucking something."

Allie's past wasn't the same as Brett's. She couldn't understand this. "Didn't her parents love her?"

"I can't see how Carl could have, but her mother did. Her mother was just scared of Carl, so she tried to look the other way. If you could've just seen her at Liza's funeral, you woulda known that much at least. The looks she gave Carl . . ." Jen shrugged. "I think maybe she knew something. But maybe she didn't. Maybe she just wished she had done something, anything, to make the years Liza had better. Happier."

"Knew something?" Brett asked.

"Knew that I didn't do it. I mean, for chrissakes, I loved Liza. Maybe she knew who did do it."

"You think it was Carl," Allie said. Not a question.

"Yeah. I don't know why or how, but I think he did it. And that's the real reason he went on such a preaching rampage — that he suddenly realized he could pin it on me." Brett wanted to say something, anything, but didn't know what. Jen seemed to realize this, so she let out a little grin. "Now you two tell me something, what's it like these days?" The first sign of real life appeared in her washed-out eyes.

"What do you mean?" Allie said.

"I mean — the gay nineties. Around here, people come and go and so I hear things, from them and the TV and I read a lot, but ..." She shrugged.

"It's a lot of two steps forward, two steps back. For instance, Colorado is now considered the hate state."

"Then it's a fitting place for Carl Swanson to be."

An hour later, when Allie and Brett were leaving the prison, Allie took Brett's hand. "I like her a lot," Allie said, clearly enjoying the bright sunlight, especially after having been "just visiting."

"I do too," Brett replied. They had both ended up talking with Jen about gay life in the nineties, and doing some comparison to the sixties and they had even promised to come back.

Brett checked her watch. "Shit," she said, "we'd better get a move on if we're gonna see both Jackie McFarley and Elise today." Both women lived in Detroit suburbs that were just a few minutes' drive from each other.

She was filled with a mixture of fear and excitement as they barreled down the highway from Jackson to Bloomfield Hills. She was slightly afraid of running into one of her old associates, yet there was a certain thrill to it as well.

She had to admit that the entire Liza Swanson scenario was strangely compelling, but she wasn't sure if it was just because it gave her something to work on, a reason to get up in the morning, or if there were some other, deeper reason that connected her to the unlucky young woman.

"Shit! Every time I think I can forget Liza, something else comes up!" Elise Galliano, nee Swanson, exclaimed when they told her their purpose. The Gallianos were obviously quite well off; not only was the house huge, eight bedrooms at least, but it was located in the very best part of the exclusive Bloomfield Hills and sat on about an acre of land.

Allie raised an eyebrow at the language. "Anything you might have to say would be most helpful and appreciated."

"Well, fuck, ya got me goin' now, so you might as well come in," Elise slurred, clearly already intoxicated, although it wasn't even noon yet. Brett looked around as they sat on the couch and decided that Elise's forte was not housekeeping. "Can I get you anything to drink?" Elise asked offhandedly as she headed to the kitchen.

"No, thanks," Allie said. Brett shook her head. She didn't like this room, though she'd guess it had probably cost a fortune to decorate it with glass topped coffee and end tables, thick pale carpeting, textured white paint and white sofas and chairs.

About the only color in the room came from the godawful paintings that were obviously not from Kmart, but were not in Brett's taste with their random splashes of color she knew was supposed to mean something, although she could never figure out what. She liked her art simple and understandable, not these random splotches and splashes that some people thought were a sign of true artistic genius. She figured most people who owned these things thought they'd show they had taste and artistic appreciation, even though they probably didn't understand or like them any better than she.

Elise came back in with a drink Brett knew was at least three shots of scotch on the rocks.

"So whatcha wanta know?" Elise sank back in the armchair and took a large swallow of her drink. "That I woulda preferred it if Jen McDonald had sliced off my arm, or my leg, or both? That I would've missed them a helluva lot less? That's the truth. When Jen killed her, she killed all that was good about me."

Allie said, "Well, that's not what we heard —"

"That's because people didn't know shit! Liza was the people person. Me, I was happy in a corner with a goddamned book. She made me do things — little shit — like go to the store or the park. She saved me from myself. She wouldn't let me live my life in a fuckin' corner." She toasted them with her glass. "In case you don't know, I'm the one who took after our dear ol' Mom. Neither of us does anything, we're too fuckin' scared to. Liza took after Dad. Big, bold and larger than life."

"You miss her a lot," Brett empathized, she couldn't see how someone could talk like Elise did and survive in this neighborhood. When she had first seen the house she assumed Elise had risen out of the smalltown mentality, but of course her large alcohol consumption was probably affecting her behavior with them. Still, it didn't make much sense.

"Hell, yes," Elise responded to Brett's question. "I didn't know what to do without her. I mean, we did almost everything together — well, up until Jen we did. But even then, she didn't exclude me. A lot of times it was my own doing that I wasn't with them. Even on that last day, she asked me to cut class with them."

"Why didn't you?" Allie asked.

"I was afraid I'd get into trouble. Pure and fuckin' simple — I was afraid of the principal's office. I was such a shittin' little goody-two-shoes."

"You don't blame yourself, do you?" Allie said, probably worried.

"If I'd only cut class with her ..." Elise trailed off. "Maybe I could've stopped Jen ..."

"You're convinced it was Jen, then?"

"I know it was."

"But even stopping her that day, she would've just come back," Allie said.

"You don't understand. Liza and I were two halves of the same whole. We made our decisions together. I could've warned her away from Jen, if I had any real indication ... I mean, like I never woulda given that Tom Ringer a second glance, except that Liza talked me into it."

"But you broke up with Tom."

"Yeah. After we moved to Colorado. Dad introduced me to Jack ..."

"Jack?" Allie interjected.

"Charles Jackson Galliano the second. Everybody calls him Jack. I guess my dad and his dad were old buddies ..." She stood and picked a picture up off a table Brett hadn't previously noticed. "That's him," she said, handing them the picture in its glossy metal frame.

The first thing most people would've noticed about the picture was the perfect picture of marital bliss it presented. The first thing Brett noticed was a faint resemblance to the old police drawing of the vagabond hippie.

"And your father introduced you to him?" Brett repeated, thinking that Carl had been seen talking with the stranger.

"Yeah," Elise replied, simply.

"Had you ever seen him before?" Allie asked.

"No, why?" Allie and Brett exchanged glances: Elise appeared to be telling the truth. Either they were imagining things, or something very strange was going on.

"Jack does quite well, I take it?" Brett said, glancing at the other photos on the table. There was a picture of Jack, another guy about his age and an older man Brett assumed was his father. Maybe a picture of him with his father and brother?

"Yeah, he does all right — comes from money." Elise shrugged. There seemed to be no love lost between her and Jack. "That's Jack, his brother Vinnie and his father," she said, indicating the other picture on the table.

"Is he close to his brother?"

Elise laughed a dry laugh. "Not really, his brother's in charge now that his Dad's so old, so Jack's always gotta be kissin' up to him. One little mistake and Jack's cut off."

Allie picked up a little statuette and rubbed some of the dust off it.

"We've thought about getting a cleanin' woman," Elise said, not defensively, "but Jack doesn't want some stranger diggin' through his shit — and I just don't care. We have help come in when there's a party, and that's about it."

138

The phone rang. Elise stood up to answer it and Brett watched her. She could almost see the woman try to push aside her drunken stupor.

The phone rang three times before she finally took a deep breath and picked it up. "Galliano residence," Elise said into the phone, in a very prim and proper manner. "Delia, my dear — it has been such a long time!" Brett studied Elise as she spoke on the phone, her face a mask of concentration as she carefully enunciated each syllable to avoid slurring. "That would be simply marvelous!" Elise seemed to be a different person, even in the way she glanced at her watch. "Very well, three o'clock at the club. I'll see you then."

Elise turned around to see both Brett and Allie silently assessing her. "It's a fuckin' façade — my entire life since Liza's death has been nothin' more than a fuckin' joke."

"Are you happy?" Allie asked as Elise escorted them to the door.

Elise turned and looked at her. "What do you think?"

"No."

As Allie and Elise exchanged looks, Brett quickly jotted her name and number on a small card, which she handed to Elise. "I know you're very busy and all . . ." she began.

"Yeah, right," Elise retorted.

"But if you think of anything else — any little anecdote or incident . . ."

"What was it you said you were doin' again?"

"Well, it's rather hard to explain in just a few sentences, but essentially we're doing histories of a lot of different murders and deaths in the past few decades, and the effects these incidents had on the people who lived to tell about it. It's about how crime doesn't just affect those directly involved."

"And this case especially interests us," Allie began, "because it's the only clear-cut case we've found prior to the nineties of a lesbian lover's triangle."

"Humph," Elise said, nonplussed.

"And I must admit," Brett said, "this case is also interesting in that we recently purchased your old house in Alma." Somehow she was hoping to get Elise's attention and help, and nothing else seemed to work.

Elise gave her an unreadable look, glanced at Allie and opened the front door.

"Shit!" Brett exclaimed, as she swiftly drove the Explorer to Ferndale, the city in which she and Allie had first met about six years previously. "She didn't give us shit!"

"That was not what I expected," Allie admitted glumly. "I expected some little cowering, timid woman. Not some drunken, foul-mouthed," she paused, as if considering the word, "bitch."

"And did you get a load of that house? I wonder what the hell Jack does for a living and what was that shit about his brother being in control now?"

"I guess it's back to the drawing board."

"What do you mean by that?" Brett asked.

Allie turned and smiled at her, frustration showing through the smile. "I mean that we don't have enough to confront Swanson yet."

"Oh, honey, the fat lady ain't sung yet. We still

140

have Jackie McFarley," Brett replied, holding onto her hope, even though she didn't feel especially hopeful.

"But what is his wife gonna know about it all?" Allie replied, echoing Brett's own concerns.

Brett stared at the road, her mind quickly flipping their quandary over and over again. "We should still go see the Swansons," she said finally. "But we'll keep with our story — to the letter — in case Elise calls them. It'll also give us a chance to talk to their neighbors and friends."

"What do you think we'll find?"

"I don't know, but it's the only lead we've got," Brett answered, even as she began to wish that Liza would wake her again tonight, but this time with something tangible she could put her hands on.

CHAPTER TWELVE

"I think George would've really liked to talk with you," Jackie McFarley said as they sat in her living room, sipping soda. "It just seems right that I should talk to you for him." Unlike Elise's overdone home, or the McDonalds rather expensive setting, Jackie McFarley's Ferndale home, in a nice family-oriented neighborhood, was a place that Brett could feel comfortable in, with its wooden tables and shelves, and simple striped sofa and loveseat. Even the paintings were simple landscapes of beautiful mountains and lakes, things that Brett could understand and enjoy.

"I just want you to know how much we appreciate this," Allie was saying to Jackie.

"No — I should be the one thanking you!" Jackie replied.

"What do you mean by that?" Brett asked, her ears prickling with interest.

Jackie quickly checked her watch. "Jessie and Jamie, our daughters, should be here any moment — they were coming straight over after work. But I guess I can begin at the beginning, and they can help fill in the blanks after." She got up and picked up a family picture from an end table. She handed it to Allie. Allie took it, and exchanged glances with Brett.

"That may be a good idea," Brett, baffled, told Jackie as she looked at the picture in its oak frame. Whatever could this woman have to say?

"I was just twenty-five when I met George," Jackie began. "He was already forty-five. Needless to say, my folks flipped when we got hitched. But I think they came to know and love him as much as I did. He was such a sweet man, and a good father."

"When did you meet him?" Allie asked.

"It was January of sixty-eight. But we dated for a full year before we got married the following January."

"So he moved down here . . ." Brett began.

"Right after the trial." Jackie nodded. "Yes. When I first met him, you could tell that deep down inside, he was troubled. But he wouldn't talk about it. I think that's one of the reasons I was first attracted to him."

"Did he ever tell you about it?" Brett asked,

worried that perhaps Jackie didn't really know anything worth telling.

"Yes," Jackie said. She sat on the coffee table facing them. "But only under extreme pressure. When we were dating, people would occasionally call his apartment, and, well, he was downright rude to them. It shocked me. It didn't happen often, maybe three or four times during that year. Well, he would never tell me anything about it, and when I married him, I hoped it was just a fluke, and not a real part of him. But it continued after we got married."

"So what did you do about it?" Allie asked, as Brett tried to draw her own conclusions.

"We were married a few months, and one day I answered the phone and it was a writer wanting to speak to George. Well, I asked him why," Jackie said, with eyebrows raised, as if this was the only thing she could've done. "And the writer asked me who I was, and I told him, and he asked if George had ever discussed the Liza Swanson case with me."

"Had he?" Brett asked eagerly, hoping she'd get to the point and give them the dirt.

"No, he hadn't," Jackie replied frankly. "He hadn't said a word about it — never even mentioned her name." She studied Brett and Allie's faces. "You have to think I'm a moron, but the George McFarley I married was a construction worker. At that point, he had never mentioned one word about what he did before that."

"So did you ask him?" Allie took a sip of her soda.

"Hell, yes, I did," Jackie said with a grin. "And that's when he finally admitted that those half-dozen or so calls had all been from reporters and writers and that he didn't want to talk with them because they didn't understand and didn't want to."

"Was that all he said?" Brett asked.

"At that point, yes. But over the next two years, I slowly learned that he had been the constable in a small town, and there had been a murder. He was involved in the investigation but wasn't allowed to run it. And, most importantly, the outcome was such that he wondered why he had ever been interested in the law in the first place."

"He wondered if there was any justice left in the world," Allie said slowly.

Jackie looked at her. "You understand," she said, nodding. "It took me quite a while to understand, really understand, just what he meant by that."

"It's tough to explain to someone who's never been there," Allie said thoughtfully.

"And you have," Jackie said. Not a question.

"And I have."

Brett sat watching the two women look into each other's eyes in a sort of communion. A dawning wave of realization began to sweep across her — she had known that the deaths of her best friend and parents had only increased Allie's passion in the law, her passion for "Truth, Justice and the American Way," but she had never fully understood the dynamics. She now realized there was more than just the deaths they had to heal from. "I always thought truth and justice were bought and sold by the highest bidder," she said, breaking the silence.

"All too often they are," Jackie said somberly.

"Justice might be, but the truth never changes," Allie argued.

Jackie looked between the two women with a grin. "Are you two very good friends?"

"Yes, why?" asked Brett, clueless.

"It just must be interesting to have two such very different viewpoints and philosophies."

Just then, the front door opened and two women entered. Jessie and Jamie McFarley were identical twins, both with long, wavy dark hair, slender builds and vivid green eyes. From a distance, Brett thought she may be faced with more Storm lookalikes, but that was not the case. Their skin was much lighter than hers had been, their features softer and less defined. Plus, they were a bit shorter and their movements had a more outdoorsy feel to them.

"Jessie's car's in the shop," Jamie said to her mother, "so I picked her up on my way home from work."

As Jackie introduced them to Brett and Allie, Jamie took Brett's hand and held it just a moment too long. Brett looked up into her green eyes and Jamie returned her look. After the introductions, Jamie, who was wearing a suit with a skirt sat on the sofa and Jessie, who was wearing jeans and a sweatshirt, sat on the living room floor at her feet. Jamie was an engineer at Ford and Jessie worked in the creative department at an ad agency.

"Anyway," Jackie continued, once everyone was settled. "Then the girls were born," she said, with a smile at the twins. "And George became the ideal father, it was as if the girls helped put pieces back into his puzzle. But then one day, when they were about ten, we were camping, and he was watching them from a distance."

"Dad always loved camping and backpacking . . ." Jessie put in.

"And anything else to do with the outdoors," Jamie said. It was obvious to Brett that George was where they had gotten their athleticism from.

"And I heard him say," Jackie continued, "under his breath, 'So much like Liza and Elise.' Obviously, I didn't understand, but the name Liza rang a bell with me. So I asked him about it. He told me that Liza and Elise were twins in Alma, where he used to live. And that from a distance, Jamie and Jessie looked a lot like them. Even then, I knew this bothered him, and, I suspected, it had bothered him since they were born."

"Dad was great — always very understanding and nonjudgmental," Jessie offered.

"I felt I could tell him anything, and he'd understand," Jamie added. "But when we were in high school, one of the girls we hung out with happened to be a lesbian."

"And he seemed really worried about it," Jessie said. "I mean, he was never one of those hate-mongers or anything, so it took us totally by surprise."

"Even I noticed he was really on edge about it," Jackie said. "And George and I both knew gay people, so I couldn't figure it out."

"Then one night, when we got home from school," Jessie said, "he was sitting here with this big box of papers."

"I always believed that George and I each needed some of our own space and privacy," Jackie explained. "So he had a trunk he kept his personal things in. And this box was in the trunk. The only thing in the trunk."

147

"Anyway," Jessie continued, glaring at her mother, "there he was, with all these old newspapers and stuff . . . And we came in, and he told us to sit down because he had something to tell us. He said that in all his life, he only regretted one thing, and that one thing was something that he hadn't really discussed with anyone in almost twenty years."

Jackie said, "He wanted to explain why he acted the way he did about Kathy."

"Kathy was the lesbian?" Allie asked.

"Yes, she was the lesbian," Jamie said. Brett looked at her and saw a twinge of curiosity and excitement.

"And that's when he told us about Liza and Elise and the Swansons and Jen," Jackie went on. "I assume you know most of the facts of the matter, so I won't go into those. But he said that he was afraid he was going to suffer some sort of universal retribution because of all the things he might've done but didn't."

"He was worried about us," Jamie clarified. "That we were dark-haired twins and now had a lesbian friend."

"I mean," Jessie clarified, "I was sad that he was worried, but I was also curious as hell. I mean, here he goes weaving this tale of a small town in the sixties, with a murder, and a lesbian love triangle, and a preacher and . . . And, well, you get the picture — wouldn't you have been curious?" Brett nodded her reply, even as she continued to glance at Jamie, who reciprocated her look with a warm smile.

"I asked George what he might've done," Jackie said, leaning back. "And that's when he told us that he'd just shared the official story. That he didn't believe Jenny McDonald killed Liza, that he didn't believe any of the kids who said they were dating Liza."

"And that he didn't believe a word Carl Swanson said," Jamie broke in.

"Did he say anything else?" Brett asked.

"You mean, things he could prove."

"Yes."

"He started the investigation by searching for some stranger," Jessie said. "A stranger that a lot of people had seen, and a few had seen talking with Carl. Dad had even seen the guy around town, although he didn't notice anything particularly peculiar about him."

"So he thought it was the stranger?" Allie asked.

"George thought the stranger played into it," Jackie said. "But he wasn't sure how. He had tried to keep himself from taking the easiest way out."

"You know," Jamie clarified, "the old 'it can't be anyone I know' routine."

"But he was suspicious of the way the guy just vanished," Jessie added.

"Then who did he think did it?" Brett asked, curious.

"Carl Swanson," Jamie replied, when neither Jessie nor Jackie said anything. "He never thought Liza was such a klutz as the Swansons had the whole town believing."

"He thought Carl was beating her," Jessie filled in.

"But back in those days, we didn't talk about such things," Jackie added.

"So he had a motive," Allie said.

"Yes," Jessie replied. "Or so he thought. He figured Liza threatened to tell, and then Carl shut her up. But he couldn't prove it."

149

"They never did find a murder weapon," Jamie said. "But he discovered that Carl did have the opportunity . . ."

"Because he took a long lunch that day," Brett said, beating her to the punch with a smile. "Then why didn't he look into that further?"

"He tried," Jackie said, "but Carl's car had had a quick fix-up job done on it, although they couldn't tell when it had happened. And that alone wasn't enough to pursue him much further without more reason, especially since he was the preacher and it was a small town. Basically his reputation was his alibi."

"That's fucked up," Brett said in frustration.

"There were a few of Carl's parishioners who said they saw him at his broke-down car but couldn't say why they didn't stop to help him."

"But did you know," Jessie excitedly said, "that Dad tried to investigate Carl's past?"

"And the man didn't exist," Jamie finished, turning around to stare at Brett again.

"What do you mean?" Brett asked.

Jackie looked at them. "He had no past. Carl Swanson didn't exist. His entire existence was based on a lie."

"George thought that he was hiding from someone," Jackie said, "Or some thing."

"So why didn't he say something?" Brett cried out in frustration and anger.

"George didn't know for sure until the trial began," Jackie began. "You see, after the trail on the stranger died, the town was still crying for vengeance. So it seems Carl grabbed the quickest suspect — Jenny McDonald. And someone paid a pretty penny to keep all the papers from saying anything about anything.

George tried to tell the police, he tried to tell the papers, but it led nowhere." She got up from her perch on the coffee table and headed to the kitchen.

"Justice, bought and sold to the highest bidder," Brett exhaled. Allie looked at her, her eyes clouding over. She knew all about having no past, all about paying off people to do what you wanted them to.

"That's why Dad didn't want to talk with any writers after the trial." There was sadness in Jessie's voice. "Because they wouldn't listen when they might have done some good."

"And because they probably still wouldn't listen," Jamie added. "Everyone claimed it was because a few of the parishioners could hold up his alibi."

"And so a young girl becomes an old woman behind bars," Brett said, thinking of the gray in Jen's hair, and the wrinkles that were only just beginning.

Jackie returned with a plate of chocolate chip cookies she put on the coffee table. "That's why it's so important for us to talk with you. I think it's important that the truth finally come out."

Brett helped herself to a cookie and took a bite, promptly swallowing it the wrong way. As she burst out coughing, Allie shot her a concerned look until she motioned that it was all right.

"I'll get you some water," Jamie offered, springing to her feet. Brett followed her to the kitchen. As soon as she had her water, the coughing subsided. She turned to rejoin the others in the living room, thinking about how she and Carl did have one thing in common: Neither had a past.

"Sam?" Jamie said, placing a gentle hand on Brett's arm while using the name Brett had introduced herself by.

151

"Yes?" she replied, turning around. Jamie took a step toward her.

"Um, well." She looked down at her feet, then blurted out, "I was just wondering how long you've been a writer, 'cause I always wanted to write a book, and, well . . ." She looked up into Brett's eyes with brilliant green eyes.

Brett felt a small flame burst out inside her stomach. Her body felt like an electrical current ran through it. She wasn't used to such blatant, unprovoked attention from such a good-looking woman she didn't know. Not lately, at least.

She let her gaze drop, slowly tracing Jamie's shapely body, from the way her shirt billowed out over her breasts, to the look of her legs in the silk stockings. She felt a crooked grin began to wind its way over her face as she went into autopilot and the old Brett Higgins came to the forefront.

Jamie reached over to finger Brett's collar. She sighed lightly and looked back into Brett's eyes. "I am really attracted to you," she whispered huskily.

Brett reached up to take Jamie's hands from her collar, holding them briefly before releasing them. She wasn't Brett Higgins anymore; she was Samantha Peterson, a happily married woman whose beautiful lover sat just in the next room.

"I have to admit, I am sorely tempted," Brett replied, studying Jamie's innocent face. How could it be possible that Jamie was just a year or so younger than she herself was?

"But?" Jamie asked, a sad, half-teasing look on her face.

"But I am madly in love with the woman sitting

on your couch," Brett said, thinking of Allie — her Allie, with her heart of truth and love of life.

"I was worried about that," Jamie paused. "But you have Mom's number if there are ever any problems in never-never land," she added coyly.

"I'll do that," Brett said. Boy, kids these days were sure getting more direct. "Do Jessie and Jackie know about you?" she asked as they headed toward the living room.

"Jess does, but I haven't gotten around to telling Mom yet."

"Doesn't matter how cool your folks are — it's always a biggie."

"You're telling me!"

A few minutes later, as Brett and Allie were leaving, Brett wrote her name and phone number on a piece of paper.

"If you think of anything else . . ." she began, extending the paper to the three women.

"We'll give you a call," Jamie replied, taking the paper as her fingers gently brushed Brett's.

CHAPTER THIRTEEN

"I just have this gut feeling that the hippie vagabond actually means something in all of this," Brett mused aloud as they drove home.

"Did you notice the McFarleys referred to him as the stranger?" Allie asked, resting her head against Brett's shoulder.

"Yeah. I kinda guessed that a local paper coined the term 'hippie vagabond' and it caught on, so the McFarleys, who weren't there then, didn't get their brains seeped in it. But we still don't have a weapon, and I really don't like the scenario the McFarleys presented . . ."

"What do you make of Elise's hubby?" Allie asked, referring to his resemblance to the elusive "hippie vagabond."

"I've been thinking about that all day, and about the only thing I can come up with is that she just didn't see the newspapers. She doesn't know he looks like the first suspect in the case. Either that, or so many people have referred to it that she no longer even bothers considering it."

"Hold on, Brett," Allie said, suddenly sitting up and looking at her. "Carl is seen talking with the stranger, but he denies it. The stranger disappears. Then, a few years later, Carl introduces a man who looks just like the stranger to Elise, and she marries him."

"So you don't think it's a coincidence."

"I'm saying it's a possibility."

"But then who is Charles Galliano the second, what does he have to do with what happened to Liza, and does any of this explain why Carl Swanson doesn't have a past?" Brett was frustrated. There were still too many loose ends.

"These and other exciting questions to be answered on the next thrilling episode of *The Killing of Liza Swanson*," Allie teased with a grin, until Brett gave her a glare. "Okay, so maybe Jack had something on Carl, maybe he knew something about his past, and that's why he was in town."

"Then maybe that's why he's married to Elise — Maybe Carl had to get her to marry Jack so Jack'd leave him alone!"

"But then why did Liza end up dead?"

"Maybe she did know something about Carl and threatened to say something, or else maybe she was Jack's first choice and she refused."

"But then how do we prove it?"

When they arrived home an hour later, the light on their machine was blinking. The first message was from Madeline. She wanted to talk with them later, but she'd just try back or stop by. The second message was from a very drunk Elise, and, in her slurred speech, she rambled on about how she had something to tell them, how she couldn't live like this any longer. They should call back tomorrow around noon, because Jack would be home tonight.

While they were in the kitchen, fixing veggie burgers for a late dinner, Madeline rang their doorbell. Allie offered her a drink and Brett threw on another burger. After some small talk, they sat down to eat. Madeline mentioned she wanted to finish reading the journal. Brett nodded, thinking that it couldn't hurt, even though she figured all the rest of the clues they'd find to this situation lay in the here and now, not in the dusty pages of the old book.

Suddenly, they heard a loud thud from the living room.

They jumped up to investigate. One of Allie's favorite paintings had fallen off the wall. They decided it must've just been the house settling that threw off the balance of the nail, except that they couldn't find the nail. The picture was undamaged though, which was a good thing, because Allie

156

would've been upset. The painting, depicting a forest with light shining through it from above, had come from her parents' house.

"Well, hell," Allie said, searching the floor behind the couch for the nail, which must've, somehow, managed to pop out. She and Brett pulled the couch forward to look, but it was nowhere to be seen. Madeline pulled all the cushions off the sofa. They still couldn't find it.

"We can deal with it in the morning," Brett said as she swallowed the rest of her veggie burger.

"No, we can't," Allie snapped. "I want to hang it up now. If we don't put it up now, it probably won't get done for weeks, and I am not tripping over this damn thing for the rest of the month."

Brett thought Allie was being silly but once the woman got on a roll there was no stopping her. "Well, then, we need a nail and a hammer."

"No, we need about three nails and a hammer," Allie corrected. "I want this thing to stay up this time. Where are they?"

"Huh?" Brett was embarrassed.

"The hammer and nails?"

"In the garage by the workbench," Brett replied, rubbing her temples. "One nail should do the trick — this thing doesn't weigh that much." She gently hefted the picture.

"I'll get them," Allie said, leaving for the garage.

"I'm sorry, Madeline," Brett shrugged. She didn't know what was possessing Allie.

Madeline gestured awkwardly.

Allie banged into the house. "Samantha Peterson!" Allie cried.

"What'd I do now?" Brett said defensively.

"You know damned well I don't appreciate your leaving butts lying around!" Allie threw the hammer and nails onto the floor.

"Where?"

"You know damned well where — by the workbench in the garage."

"Huh?"

"Don't play dumb with me." Allie took Brett by the arm and led her out toward the garage.

Madeline hesitated, as if she were considering leaving, but then followed them. Brett muttered another apology to her.

"There!" Allie cried triumphantly, pointing to the butt lying on the floor in the garage. Brett reached down to pick it up.

"It's not even my brand . . ." Brett began as she stood with the butt, but then she noticed Allie and Madeline weren't looking at her, they were looking at the workbench. She turned to see what was so interesting and saw, in the big scrawled letters she had found in the journal a few nights before:

? Known
Unknown

The letters were haphazardly written in the dust on the counter top. Brett slowly sank to the floor as the words came back to her.

"Honey, what is it?" Allie said, kneeling beside her.

"The other night, the cigarette . . ." She held up the butt.

Allie took it from her and examined it. "There's no brand name on it." Allie handed it to Madeline, who accepted it, but looked instead at Brett.

"What happened the other night?"

"She said 'I know about loss.' "

Allie started to speak, but Madeline held up her hand and crouched in front of Brett. "Who said that?"

Brett looked up at Madeline. "I don't know. It was a voice that woke me up." She proceeded to fill Madeline and Allie in on the events that led up to the cigarette being left on the garage floor, intentionally leaving out the epilogue in which Storm appeared.

"So now the ghost is a litterbug," Allie said, going to toss out the butt.

Madeline stopped her and took the butt. She said to Brett, "I think she wanted you to come in here."

"Why? Because it's a mess?" Brett said, standing.

"There's something here she wants you to see."

They looked around the garage, which had at one time, obviously, been someone's work area. Not only was there the workbench connected to the wall, but there were also additional shelves, covered with a thin layer of dust and grime. The floor was covered with spilled paint, oil and dried mud. Brett was surprised the realtors or former inhabitants hadn't cleaned it.

"Carl Swanson must be an anal retentive asshole," she said, tapping a wall.

"What do you mean by that?" Allie asked.

"Who else would've paneled their frickin' garage?" Brett gestured toward the plywood that had been mounted on the walls to cover the supports and beams.

"Do you smell something?" Madeline asked, sniffing.

Brett didn't smell anything, but something about the garage gave her an odd chill.

"I think it's just musty and dusty," Allie said as she led them back to the house.

When they entered the living room, hammer and nails in hand, the picture was already hanging on the wall, the couch neatly positioned underneath it.

When Madeline finally left that night, Brett and Allie went upstairs to their bedroom. Once inside the room, Allie put her hand over Brett's, preventing her from turning on the lights. "No." She paused. "Brett, you said you know about loss . . ."

Brett suddenly realized Allie knew her far too well. Allie had to be thinking about Storm. Brett picked her up easily and laid her down on the bed. She gently brushed Allie's ear with her tongue so the warmth ran through Allie's body. She loved Allie, didn't want to lose her or cause her fear over their relationship. She didn't have the words to say this, but . . .

Brett's mouth came to Allie's, her lips parted slightly, and then she was inside Allie; her tongue brushing against hers, her leg between hers, pushing against her. Allie arched up, against Brett, groaning as Brett pressed against her even harder, while their tongues tangoed further still. She couldn't let Allie know about the doubts that tortured her.

Allie reached up and pushed against Brett's shoulders, rolling her over onto her back. She sat up to straddle Brett, who smiled up at her, deftly undoing the buttons of her blouse and then the clasp on her bra, till both were undone and she could easily push them off Allie's fine, slender shoulders.

Allie sat up straight, her legs spread open over Brett, the moonlight coming in through the half-open blinds, giving the entire setting a dreamlike quality.

"You are so beautiful," Brett said, openly admiring Allie's naked form, her hands roaming up from Allie's waist, to cup her breasts, toying with her nipples, until they found her shoulders and brought Allie back down on top of her.

Allie's legs were still spread out over Brett when Brett rolled her over onto her back, again pressing into her while Allie squirmed beneath her, her need and urgency growing greater by the moment.

"Brett, oh, God, Brett," Allie moaned. "I need you so bad . . . Please . . ."

Brett knelt between Allie's legs, swiftly undoing her button-fly and pulling the jeans, underwear, socks and shoes down in one sure, swift motion, before standing and quickly pulling off her own clothes and tossing them carelessly to the side.

Flesh against flesh, body heat to body heat, they lay with each other. Allie wrapped her long legs around Brett, pulling her into her as she pulled Brett deeper into the kiss, letting her know she needed her, with a firm hand to the back of Brett's head.

Brett's hands were strong yet gentle and sensitive, knowing just how Allie liked to be touched. Brett looked up to meet her eyes, just before she brought her hand into Allie's wetness, running her fingers up and down Allie's clit, sliding through the wetness, bolted in place to this incredible intimacy.

Slowly Brett entered Allie, gliding first one then another finger into her, until she leaned down, her eyes still holding Allie's, and ran her tongue over Allie, licking up her juices before teasing back and forth and up and down.

Allie put one hand into Brett's hair, holding her tightly, bringing Brett against her tightly till Brett closed her eyes and buried her face, her tongue, in Allie. Her other hand held Brett's, connecting them further still.

"Brett!" Allie screamed, bucking her around the bed. Brett held on tightly, not losing Allie for the life of her as the mad bronco ride continued.

Gradually, the spasms slowed and then stopped, till Allie was able to start running her hands through Brett's hair, brushing it out till Brett gradually withdrew from Allie, then climbed up on top of Allie, laying her head against Allie's breast.

"I love you," Brett said.

CHAPTER FOURTEEN

"We'll have to hurry," Allie said the next morning as she hung up the phone. "Our plane leaves from Lansing in two hours." They had decided, because of time limits, to take the risk of flying from Lansing to Detroit, and even laying over, briefly, in Detroit.

"We have one phone call to make first," Brett replied, looking up from her breakfast and the morning paper.

"Yes, didn't Elise call last night?" Madeline added, looking up from the journal, which she was reading. She had stayed until late the night before and came over first thing in the morning. Brett was beginning to think she might become a permanent fixture in their home during the coming years.

"That's right!" Allie said, quickly searching for the piece of paper with Elise's phone number. When she found it, she picked up the phone, ready to dial, then hung it up again. "She said not to call until noon."

"Shit," Brett grumbled, looking at her watch. "Maybe we can call her from Detroit, or when we get to Colorado."

"That'll have to do."

They left Madeline still reading the journal.

It wasn't until Denver that they were able to call Elise. After leaving the plane, they quickly found a pay phone, and Allie dialed, holding the receiver so that Brett, too, could listen to the conversation.

They heard the phone ring once, twice, three times, before Elise answered. "Galliano residence, may I help you?"

"Yes, Elise, this is Allie Sullivan — I think you left a message on our machine last night . . ."

"Yeah, I remember," Elise replied. Brett could almost see the society matron image slide away from the woman. "Ya see, I got to thinkin' about what you said you were doin', how murders affect the survivors, and, well . . ."

"Yes?" Allie eagerly prodded.

"Ya see, without Liza, I'm not a whole person, but there's more to it than that — 'cause Liza and I were a team. We worked together. But I didn't really know how much she did for me till she died."

"What do you mean by that?"

"You ain't gonna quote me on this or anything, are you?"

164

"No, no, your anonymity is guaranteed," Allie assured her.

"After we moved to Colorado, well, Carl started payin' more attention to me. I think I had always known, deep down, what was up with him and Liza, but I had myself convinced they just didn't get along . . ."

"You mean he raped you," Allie said.

"Yes," Elise said, obviously relieved she didn't have to say it herself. She paused. "So when he introduced me to Jack — Jack with all his money and his big, flashy car — I went for it. At the time it seemed like the only escape from the hell-hole my life was."

"What do you mean you 'went for it'?"

"I mean I took the goddamned bait! But it didn't take me long to figure out that Jack is nothin' more than a goddamned faggot! And I thought I could live with that, live with bein' his cover, makin' it so he didn't embarrass his family anymore. After all, the pay ain't bad — a fuckin' mansion in Bloomfield Hills, a Porsche and a Jaguar in the garage, everythin' I could ever fuckin' want just so long as I play nice."

"So why did you decide to tell us this?"

"Because it's somethin' no one would really think about — that without Liza I'd go and make all the wrong choices — that I could so totally fuck up my life. How stupid could I be? I mean, I'm livin' here with Jack and his little parade of boy-toys — he's so messed up he can't even keep a single one of them around —"

"What went wrong that made you decide to not just keep playing nice?" Brett broke in, frustrated, wondering why Elise suddenly decided to tell her story.

165

"I found out that that motherfuckin' Carl sold me to him!"

"What?" Allie asked, patting Brett's arm.

"Okay, so it was a coupla years ago, and Jack was bringin' home another one of his little boys — which was fine with me, 'cause we sleep in different rooms and all . . . Course, nobody knows that," Elise explained. Brett could hear the sounds of Elise pouring a drink and lighting a cigarette. "But one night I go downstairs to get myself some ice cream, and I hear them carrying on in the kitchen. They're laughing and shit. Not even wantin' to know what they're doin', I'm about to go upstairs, when this little shit asks Jack about the old ball and chain. So I stop to listen, and Jack laughs and says that Carl sold me to him."

"What did he mean by that?" Allie said, but Brett grinned, she knew what Elise meant — and she had figured it out a day ago.

"That's what I wanted to know — I mean, he was fuckin' braggin' 'bout it — so the next day I ask him. Well, that little fucker looks at me with the evilest gleam in his eye and asks me why I ever could've believed that a low-life like Carl knew people like Jack and his dad. He told me he needed a cover, 'cause Charles, his dad, didn't want everybody to know he had a faggot for a son. And it just so happened that Paul Misner owed Charles a lot of money and had skipped town and changed his name. When the Gallianos found him, he agreed that one of his daughters would marry Jack, and just so long as the daughter played along, Paul could live. His first choice was Liza, 'cause he figured they'd get along, and once they were married, people'd be less likely to notice a woman having an affair with a woman as opposed to a man."

"So Carl Swanson, your father, was really Paul Misner?" Allie asked.

"Yup."

"So why didn't you leave when he told you this?"

"Where the fuck would I go?"

"And why are you telling me all this?"

Elise was thoughtful for a moment, then it rushed out in a wave of emotion. "I needed to tell someone. I don't really have no friends. I went with Jack to escape Dad, and I did. I haven't seen him since the day I got married. He writes now and then. Sends a Christmas card. I've sent Mom notes, called, trying to talk to her, but Dad always pulls the phone from her, and she wouldn't dare try to call me. These days I don't even really try anymore — 'cause I don't want to talk with that asshole. Anyway, last night I was thinkin' 'bout Liza and that her and I and Jen were gonna run away together, and we were gonna be happy, and then Liza . . ." Her voice was smothered by a sob. "And then Liza was killed and I didn't know what the fuck to do —"

"And the resemblance to the quote unquote hippie vagabond didn't disturb you at all?" Brett said, cutting her off.

" 'Hippie vagabond'?" Elise asked.

"Yeah, the fellow they first thought killed Liza," Brett replied, frowning.

"I don't know shit about that — my parents wouldn't let me near the papers, and everybody else was scared to say shit to me about it. I mean, I went into the courtroom, said my piece, then got the fuck outta there."

"So how are you so sure it was Jen?"

"Who else could it be?"

A short while later, as they pulled up in the Swansons' driveway in Aurora, Colorado, a suburb of Denver, which was just a frisbee throw from some of the most gorgeous mountains Brett had ever seen, she put the car in park and pulled the keys out of the ignition. She bent forward to pound her head against the steering wheel. She felt Allie's hand gently touch the back of her neck.

Brett looked up. "How can she be so blind?"

"Brett, honey," Allie replied, cupping Brett's cheeks. "You have to realize that the worst crimes are the ones committed by those we love — because we are supposed to be able to trust our family. When they do something bad to us, we don't know what to do. We can't accept that our father, brother, mother or sister can be so evil."

"But she already knows he's evil," Brett argued, even as she knew in her heart that what Allie said was true.

"But he's the man who raised her. Underneath it all, he's still her daddy. And to top it off, she's been so brainwashed with religion that she sees her father, the preacher, as being only a few steps away from God. Even if her head knows he's bad, her heart still won't believe it." She paused, looking into Brett's eyes. "That's what makes incest such a mind-blowing crime: we are attacked by those we have been trained to think love us, and that we love in return."

"And the real reason she won't mess up Jack's

little game is because then her dearly beloved father will get blown away." Brett glanced up over the house and at the mountains, with their sprinkling of trees and caps of white as Allie sadly nodded her head. "But then why'd she tell us about it?"

"Maybe she was feeling regret, or maybe she just got drunk — y'know how obsessed and such you can get when you're drinking . . ." Allie let her sentence trail off.

Brett shook her head in disbelief and got out of the car. Allie stood by her side as she rang the doorbell. As they waited for an answer, Brett took a step back to study the house.

"They must pay the preachers in this town . . ." Just then the front door opened. She wasn't sure what she expected, but it wasn't this haggard-looking woman.

"Yes?" Margaret Swanson said with a voice that was a cut between a growl and a creak. Her slight frame was dressed in old polyester pants, dirty pink slippers, a prim blouse and an old cardigan sweater tossed about her shoulders, which were caving in, much like the woman they belonged to. In fact, all of Margaret Swanson's being seemed to be closing in on itself, as if it wanted to disappear in a puff of smoke.

Allie quickly introduced Brett and herself, and Margaret looked down to the ground. She shrugged and let them into the house.

"Elise called to tell me you were coming," she said as they sat in the kitchen. She looked around nervously, as if she were afraid of something. "She doesn't call much anymore, so I guess I should thank you for getting her to speak to me."

"You had a falling out?" Allie asked, trying to

appear concerned as Brett wandered around the kitchen.

"No, not really. I just haven't seen her since the day she married Jack. Of course, I write and send her birthday and Christmas cards, but she never writes back." She again looked around nervously. Brett was beginning to see the pattern. Margaret wouldn't admit that it was Carl who wouldn't let her communicate with her daughter because she was afraid of him. He probably also took what letters or cards Elise sent and kept them.

"But it doesn't matter because our world had fallen apart the day Liza was killed. We had to move from Alma because of the memories." She wiped at her tears with a well-used tissue she had in the sleeve of her sweater. "I was born in Alma and planned on dying in Alma. But nothing ever happens quite the way you expect." She gave a resigned sigh. She probably knew who killed Liza and that's why she wasn't fighting to keep Elise near, why she no longer cared about herself or anything else.

"Didn't you think it rather strange that Elise's husband Jack so closely resembles the man they originally thought killed Liza?" Brett asked.

"Elise said you were doing a study of the aftereffects of murder. She didn't say you were planning to re-open that entire can of worms." Margaret jumped up, but she wasn't indignant, she was scared. She glanced around quickly before whispering, "Girls, I love my daughter, and I'll do anything to keep her safe. I failed with the first, but I won't fail again."

Suddenly, from the back of the house, came a big, booming "Margaret! Where is my collar?!"

Brett and Allie turned to face the man who entered the kitchen. Standing about six feet tall, Carl Swanson was a heavyset, imposing man with a bolt of white hair neatly brushed back from his eyes. Brett felt swallowed alive by the vivid green eyes that searched her own.

The eyes looked familiar and, with a shock, Brett suddenly realized where she had seen them before: in a recent dream. They belonged to a man she first assumed was her father, because he was chasing her. In her dream she rolled over and saw an unfamiliar face. That unfamiliar face belonged to the man who now stood before her.

"You can go now," Margaret Swanson whispered, afraid as she looked at her husband.

"You don't know shit about interviewing people," Allie said several hours later on the plane home. They had gone on to try to question the Swansons' neighbors, but they had been either tight-lipped or members of the Carl Swanson fan club. It was the tight-lipped ones who got their interest.

"Whaddya mean?" Brett said, sullenly, silently telling herself that Margaret Swanson wouldn't have revealed anything anyway, not with the way Carl controlled her.

"You can't blurt out questions they don't want to hear," Allie explained. "You have to play with them first."

"Well, shit." Brett sighed. "I wanted the answer to that question." She figured she already knew it, but didn't like to go on instinct alone. She wanted everything verified each step of the way.

"And you didn't get it because you shot it out as she was crying for her hometown and her dead daughter."

"Actually," Brett said as she sat back in her seat' "I think I got my answer."

CHAPTER FIFTEEN

That night, Brett and Allie arrived home to find Madeline cleaning the garage. There were a few garbage bags out front, all the shelves were clean, and Madeline was just finishing mopping the floor.

"Normally I wouldn't mop a garage floor — but this one was just too dirty for a mere broom," Madeline explained as she looked up from her chore.

"Wow," Brett said, blinking as she walked through the garage.

"It's a pity, though," Madeline said, propping her mop up against the workbench. "Somebody leaned a few things that were a little too heavy against these walls." She indicated a few holes that were punched in the plywood.

"I can't thank you enough!" Allie exclaimed, hugging Madeline.

"Allison," Madeline replied, pushing her away. "It's nothing."

"But —"

"I am worried, however, that you will have to pull all this plywood out of here. I'm afraid that something crawled into a wall and died."

"Why do you think that?" Brett asked, curious, studying the walls.

"I can't seem to get rid of that strange smell."

Brett and Allie sniffed the air. "I don't smell anything," Brett said, shrugging.

"There's something — but I just can't place it," Allie added as she walked around, still sniffing.

"Regardless," Madeline said, leading them out as she turned off the lights. "I didn't find a thing, although I am positive there is something here that Liza wants us to find."

"It could've just been a dream," Brett declared as they entered the house.

"Brett, darling," Madeline said. "I love you to death, but your skepticism is driving me to drink."

"Brett," Allie said, wrapping her arms around her lover's waist, "if it was just the visitation, I might buy that — but the visitation *and* the picture that fell off the wall?"

"Maybe there was something bad in our veggie burgers last night —" Allie cut her off with a kiss. As the kiss lengthened, Madeline cleared her throat.

"Children, I don't mind that whatsoever, but I

174

really, really want to know what happened in Colorado." And so the three women sat sipping wine in the living room while Allie filled Madeline in on their findings. Brett paced the room restlessly. At one point, Allie broke off her narrative to come stand behind Brett, who stood staring out the window. With not even that much of a breeze, Madeline's huge oak tree was sprinkling a layer of red, yellow and orange leaves across their lawn.

"What's the matter honey?"

"It feels like rain," Brett replied, shivering.

Madeline joined them at the window. "It's a beautiful night out."

Madeline and Allie returned to sit on the couch, and Brett lay in the fetal position next to Allie, with her head on Allie's lap. She almost felt like dozing off as she listened to the hum of conversation and Allie gently stroked her hair . . .

They still didn't know enough, although they had solved the impossible puzzle of tracking down the hippie vagabond thirty years after the fact. Brett knew Jack and his father fit in somewhere, she just wasn't sure exactly how. Something was up, somehow everything fit together, but she didn't know exactly how.

With the nagging sensation of a storm ringing around her ears, she was half-asleep imagining that she was there as Jen and Liza made love that long ago afternoon. She was there as Jen climbed out the window and told Liza she loved her. She was there as Liza walked down the stairs, unafraid, only to find —

Allie tugged at Brett's ear. "Hey," she whispered. "Are you still with us?"

Brett sat up, shaking her head. "Yeah."

"Did you hear what Madeline just suggested?"

"No, what?" Brett asked, looking at Madeline.

"I think we should do a walk-through. A reenactment, if you will."

Brett raised an eyebrow. "That's an idea. See if we can figure out how it all happened."

"Why don't you be Liza," Allie suggested, "since you seem to be in tune with her, and I'll be Carl."

"And I," Madeline said, "will watch for any inconsistencies or other items of note."

"What about Jen?" Brett asked.

"She left as soon as the front door opened," Madeline said. "So I'll play her."

"Okay," Brett replied, standing. "Where do we begin?"

"At the beginning," Madeline said frankly as she stood. "Allie, you go outside, like we discussed, and Brett, I'll go upstairs with you."

Brett lay down on the spare bed in the room that had once been Liza's.

"Now close your eyes, dear," Madeline instructed her. "And imagine it's November thirteenth, nineteen sixty-seven. It's a fall day, and you've cut class to come home and make love with Jen."

Brett tried to imagine being Liza and being with Jen, but unbidden images of Storm and Allie tumbled through her mind. "Madeline?" she asked.

"What dear?" Madeline replied, sitting on the bed.

"Do you think Allie and I are supposed to be together?"

"What makes you ask something like that?"

Brett sat up and looked at Madeline. "The other night I thought Storm had come back — and I told her I loved her . . . and I meant it."

"Did you tell Allison about that?"

Brett rolled her eyes.

"Why not?" Madeline asked, not accusing.

"Because I cheated on Allie with Storm, and vice versa."

"So how'd you end up with Allie?" Madeline asked, aware that they were going into uncharted territory. She hadn't heard too much about Brett's past.

"Someone killed Storm," Brett admitted, a tear coming to her eye.

"If that hadn't happened, how would it have ended?"

"I broke it off with Storm just before she died. I thought I loved her the wrong way for all the wrong reasons."

"And have you regretted that decision?"

"Yes. I keep asking myself if I hadn't done that, if Storm would still be alive."

"Do you really believe she would?"

Brett lay back on the bed, staring at the ceiling. "No, if she hadn't gotten killed that night, it would've been another night."

"Somebody killed her?"

"Yeah. But that leaves me wondering if I had made the right decision — if I should be with Allie, or if Storm should've been the one. It's like I knew I loved them both — but I couldn't imagine life without either of them. And they were both so young, I wasn't sure if either of them was ready for a full commitment."

Madeline looked down at her. "But you and Allie broke up for a while."

"Yeah. She found out about Storm, and I just

crumbled." Brett sat up and looked at her. "I just, I just couldn't deal with it."

"Are you sure it was they who weren't ready for commitment?"

"I was ready," Brett argued. "Sure I enjoyed playing the field, but . . ."

"Brett, I've been watching you and Allie, and, well . . ." Madeline paused, for the first time, in Brett's opinion, unsure of what she was going to say. "And do you think you deserve love? Do you feel worthy of giving love?"

"Yeah, sure," Brett grinned. "I mean, I've done some things I'm not exactly proud of, but who hasn't?"

"Brett, in response to your original question, I'll tell you that I think you'll be happy with Allie if you'll let yourself be."

Brett stared at Madeline as she flipped back in her mind to who else had said those same words. "That's what Storm said."

"Brett, as we go through life, we occasionally make mistakes and love people who don't deserve our love. But we have to learn that that was just a mistake, and that there are people out there who not only deserve our love, but will return it in kind. And one has to learn, to believe and feel, with our heads," Madeline reached over and tapped Brett's temple, then she lowered her hand to touch near Brett's heart. "*And* with our hearts."

Brett heard the downstairs door open. "Hey! You guys!" Allie yelled. "You're supposed to die down here, not up there!"

"Behave!" Madeline yelled back. "We'll be ready soon. Just wait outside until I give the signal!" They heard the downstairs door open and close again, then Madeline turned to Brett. "Just lie back and imagine . . ."

Brett lay back and tried to imagine the day, tried to imagine that she was Liza and she was with Jen, making love. She began to visualize. "I'm hot, but it's freezing outside," she said. It was as if she weren't quite herself. "But this feels so good. Oh so good." She was vaguely aware of Madeline standing to flick the lights off then on. Then she heard the downstairs door open. "Shit!" Brett whispered. "Someone's home!" Blindly, she hurried to dress and help Jen out the window, where she could climb down the trellis to the ground. They kissed, and Jen told her that she loved her.

Brett was feeling displaced, like she was being relegated to the position of bystander — like she was somebody else. She got up and went downstairs, figuring it was just Elise deciding to cut class after all. Mom wasn't due back until later, since it was the day of her big card game, and Dad always got home at 5:30, and it was nowhere near that time yet.

She walked through the kitchen and heard her father's big booming voice. The known and the unknown were colliding. She knew it was Allie standing in front of her and that she wasn't actually speaking, but she could picture Carl Swanson standing there, roaring at her, almost thirty years ago.

"Liza?" he asked, angry with her. "What're you doing home?"

"I . . . I was sick," she responded weakly. But something was wrong. There was a stranger with him. "Who are you?" she asked, straining to make out a face from the shadow standing next to Allie/Carl.

179

"I'm your father!" Allie replied, not knowing what was happening. "Carl Swanson." Brett shook her head and looked at a space just to the left of Allie.

"What's the matter?" Madeline asked, touching Brett's shoulder. Brett was grateful for the contact — it made her feel more like herself. There was still a chill creeping over her limbs, a blurriness to her vision.

"There were two people . . ." Brett said, trying to regain the memory, but it felt like a dream, a dream that was slowly seeping out of her mind like water from a sieve.

"It must've been Jack," Allie suggested, walking over to Brett.

"Yeah, I think it was," Brett said, nodding. "And I knew I was about to get beaten for cutting class, and I was afraid — I wasn't afraid until I came down and saw Carl and Jack . . ."

"So Jack was here," Allie said with a nod.

Madeline looked around. "Let's all sit down, in a circle, and try to get Liza back . . ."

"Are you suggesting a seance?" Brett asked in disbelief.

"No, not really. A seance would be to make contact with Liza and she has already contacted us — you, so that would be rather silly now, wouldn't it?" She paused and looked first at Brett, then at Allie. "Besides, most seances are shams. I was merely suggesting we attempt to enlist her aid in our endeavor."

"Madeline," Brett said, stopping her pacing and looking at the older woman, "remember, I'm butch — I believe in what's here, what's tangible. I don't deal well with other things — like emotions and ghosts and crap."

"Butch?" Allie eyed her. "Then let's try this — shut up, sit down and do as you're told."

Brett thought about arguing, but just sat down instead. Allie and Madeline joined hands and each grabbed one of Brett's hands. She felt like a jerk, this was pretty damned silly.

"It's a cold day, the wind is bitter," Madeline said. "Carl, you left work at lunchtime and said you needed to run some errands. Instead, you met Jack and brought him back here. Carl owes Jack's father money, lots of it, and Jack's been hanging around town for a few days, trying to decide which of Carl's daughters he wants. Liza's at home, upstairs making love with Jen . . ."

"The wind's coming in from the windows," Brett said. All she knew was she was suddenly feeling chilled, but strangely animated. It felt as if one of her hands were cold and wet and the other was touching an electrical outlet, as if there was a low-level current running through her body. "I know it's cold, but I'm sweating."

It was as if there was a battle going on inside Brett. She knew she had to go with it, give up control, but she had worked so hard to always be in charge that it was a struggle. Although she had learned at a young age never to show or allow fear, its wicked prongs still slowly crawled along her skin, digging deeper into her being.

Even as she knew her skin was cold, she felt a warmth begin to burn its way up from her stomach and, as it worked its way up her backbone and through her kidneys, into her lungs and heart, she began to feel tired. The room slowly began to blur and become gray. She fought to bring things into focus — first the furniture, then the walls, finally Allie — before she realized it meant her no harm.

Still, she was scared. The room had changed. It looked like the spare room, and she could clearly make out the pattern on the bedspread and the grain of the walls. And then, even as she watched, the walls changed colors. She could see the old throw rugs from twenty-nine years ago, Liza and Elise's desks cluttered with schoolwork, the old bureau . . .

Her heart began to beat even faster as anxiety rippled through her limbs. A thought exploded in her skull, screaming at her to pull out of this, telling her that she could, even as she saw Liza's naked form on the bed with Jen going down on her.

Brett looked down at herself, her jeans and sweatshirt, knowing who she was even as she seemed to step toward the bed, as if pulled by some force.

She stared down at Liza's face, memorizing each detail. So much like Storm, with her long hair draped over her shoulder and her mouth opened slightly, moaning in ecstasy . . .

Brett pulled her knee up onto the bed and in a split-second of nothingness, she leaned down toward Liza and lost herself completely. She *was* Liza.

She was rushing over the edge when she heard the car door bang in the driveway. Jen bolted upright, a look of panic crossing her face.

"Shit, someone's home," Brett heard the dreamlike voice say, even though it came from within what seemed to be herself.

The front door opened and closed. Snowy boots

were stamped against the front rug. Possibilities rushed through her mind while she and Jen hurriedly dressed: Mother, home early from her cardgame; Elise, deciding to cut class after all . . .

"You'd better get out of here," she told Jen, directing her to the window so she could climb down the trellis. Jen paused, reached over and kissed her on the lips.

"I love you," she said, before disappearing out the window to climb carefully down the icy trellis. She would run down the street to the store where she had left her car.

She went downstairs, figuring it had to be Elise. Of course, it might just be a neighbor come to borrow a cup of sugar, except all the neighbor women were playing cards across town with her mother. Regardless, Liza wasn't afraid. Crime didn't really exist in 1967 in Alma, Michigan. Even if an occasional hippie vagabond came to town looking for a hand-out as he journeyed across America, he was certain to leave once he realized nothing ever happened in Alma.

"What are you doing home?" her father bellowed at her. He had some strange man with him. Liza vaguely recalled having seen him around town with her father.

"I . . . I wasn't feeling well, so they sent me home . . ." She didn't like the stare the stranger was giving her, as if he was sizing her up, undressing her with his eyes, almost but not quite. "Who's he?" she asked, fearful of her father and the stranger, even as she tried to call up Jen's strength.

"I'm sorry, sweetie," he began, his voice softening as he looked at her. "This is Charles Galliano the second." He turned toward the man, "And Jack, this is my darling daughter Liza."

There was something wrong. She knew this before the scraggly-haired man bowed to kiss her hand, his hard whiskers brushing her hand. She knew this from somewhere deep inside her. She backed up against the wall and her breathing became heavy, anxiety rushing through her system.

"Pleased to meet you," Jack said, leering a little. Liza pulled her hand away from him. Jack looked at her, then at her dad.

Her father walked over to her and brushed his hand down her cheek. Only long-term training kept her from backing away at the male smell of him. "Sure this is the one you want?" he asked Jack.

Jack ogled her. "Yeah, she's the one." He walked over and touched her like a horse. "Nice tits. Good hips. I can see her popping out a coupla puppies . . . Keep Father happy." She let him touch her only because she was pressed against the wall.

"Then it's a deal?" Carl asked, pulling away to look at Jack. There were two of them and only one of her. She focused on Jen, protecting herself, and part of her left her body and went elsewhere.

"Tell me," Jack said to Carl, clutching her so that she rode his hip. "Which would you pick, Elise or her?"

Her father paused and Liza could see him weighing the pros and cons.

Jack saw the hesitation, threw her back against the wall and drew a switchblade. "Don't fuck with me, asshole." He backed Dad against the wall with his knife. "You have more to worry about than just my fuckin' daddy." He placed the blade tight against her father's throat.

"You're just a fuckin' faggot," her father spat.

"And you're an asshole, Paul."

Liza saw her chance. She could turn and run and, perhaps, get out of the house and over to the Jarvises', or some other safe place, before they could catch her. She could run away with Jen, grab Elise . . .

But she didn't have time to think or feel. He was her father. She reached forward and grabbed Jack, who lurched at her. The hot blade ripped across her throat. She felt it cut into her flesh, cut deep. Pain roared through her as the knife hit her larynx.

Jack's arm continued its arc and then came down to his side as he realized what he had done. He turned wild-eyed to Dad, who stood, mouth agape, still pressed against the wall, then to Liza. She clutched her throat as the sickeningly sweet, salty taste of blood filled her mouth. She started to double over as the pain coursed through her body like white-hot electricity.

The blood, on her hands, on the floor, was hers. There was too much of it.

Anger and rage crossed Jack's face as he changed his grip on the knife. "Bitch!" he screamed, bringing the knife up into her stomach, liver, kidneys, again and again and again he thrust at her, ripping through flesh, tearing her apart, his thrusts the only thing keeping her upright.

A scream roared through her ears. Everything was blurred, and then the pain gave way to a blissful numbness.

* * * * *

The pain was gone. She felt light and . . . free. She stood up with amazing ease and the room came back into focus. It was as if life was running in slow motion, though.

Visibly trembling, her father stood covered with blood, his face and skin ashen. He was looking at something on the floor. He looked up at Jack, who was sneering down. Jack threw the knife that was still dripping blood onto the floor, reached into his jacket and pulled out a gun.

The knowledge that that was her blood suddenly struck Liza. She turned to look at what the two men were staring at and saw her own bloody, mutilated body with its eyes rolled up toward the ceiling.

If she had actually been breathing, she would've stopped; if she had had a heart anymore, it would've stopped beating in that moment.

She was dead.

She wanted to cry but no longer had tears. She wanted to scream, break something, but she no longer had a body. She wanted to sit down and take her poor, torn body into her arms and comfort it.

Jack turned to her father with the gun.

"No, no . . ." he pleaded, backing away from him.

"You finish her," Jack growled, tossing him the gun. He caught it and looked at Jack in horror. "The only way I know you won't talk," Jack hissed, "is if you're in on it. Finish it, or I finish you."

With tears in his eyes, Carl turned and looked at Liza, whose blood was already sopping the carpet. He aimed and fired.

* * * * *

186

Brett was screaming, shaking as if she were in the throes of a seizure. There were hands on her, trying to grab her. She pushed them away, bringing her own hands up to defend herself as tears streamed down her face.

"Brett! Brett!" Allie yelled as Brett backed herself into a corner and slowly crumpled to the floor. Madeline stood back as Allie knelt next to Brett. "Brett, it's okay," Allie said, trying to gently stroke Brett's hair as Brett fought her off.

Suddenly she stopped. She looked up at Allie. She wiped her eyes with her sleeve.

"Are you all right?" Allie gently asked. "You're white as a ghost." This latter statement struck somewhere deep inside Brett, making her take a deep breath. Allie pulled her into her arms.

In her life, Brett had been beaten, shot at and knifed, with the scars to testify to the more successful attempts, but she had never been mutilated to such an extent.

Every part of her still remembered the intense pain as the cold metal cut through her flesh, the overwhelming fear as she realized she was going to die, the incredible anger and sadness when she realized she was dead.

She knew what she had to do. She shakily brought her aching body to its feet. "Jack left Carl to clean up the mess," she said with a certainty she couldn't claim as her own. "Carl had to hurry, because Elise would be back from school shortly. He was scared. He changed his uniform, grabbed the knife and gun, stuck it all in bags and went —" She paused, trying not to think or feel, but just to know. "He went to the garage."

187

Brett led the way out the side door and into the yard. She stopped and stared at the garage. A storm was brewing, darkening the star-filled night.

She quickly unlocked the garage door and entered, turning on the lights. The three quickly looked through the garage.

"Are you sure you didn't find anything when you were cleaning?" Allie asked Madeline.

"Honey, I would've noticed a bloody knife and gun."

Brett stood silently staring into the space in front of them. Wordlessly, she turned and left.

"The smell . . ." Allie said, glancing around. None of the panels that covered the walls was tall enough to cover the entire ten-foot expanse of wall, so in all places, two boards were cut to fit together. Madeline peered into the holes, hoping one had been created in order to dump the evidence. "This could take us all night."

Brett grabbed a crowbar from the Explorer's trunk and viciously began attacking the walls, pulling board after board down, ripping them like Jack had ripped into Liza. She knew her mission, knew what she had to do and did it. Sweat poured down her face and she yanked off her sweatshirt, the muscles in her arms straining, taking it all out on the garage.

Allie and Madeline stood back, wide-eyed, until they finally started pulling things out of Brett's way, clearing the debris and watching.

Half of the walls were torn apart, sweat dripped from Brett's brow, and the sounds weren't those of crickets or owls, but the booms as Brett ripped down board after board. She finished one and methodically moved to the next, a machine in her inexhaustible search.

She yanked the next board from the wall and a dusty garbage bag tumbled out and onto the floor. Intent on her job, Brett saw it but didn't really notice it until Allie grabbed her arm and pointed. The three women stood in silence, looking at the horrid thing in front of them.

Brett reached down and picked it up. She gingerly carried it into the house, knowing it was double bagged. She wanted to open it somewhere clean, so as to not spoil any important evidence that might be left after nearly thirty years.

When Brett opened the bag on the kitchen table, she could barely smell what was once probably a rather putrid odor. Madeline and Allie watched eagerly as Brett tore open what remained of the inner bag.

Allie wordlessly handed Brett latex gloves from under the sink. Brett looked up into her eyes and smiled. At that moment, she knew Allie was her true soulmate and that she would go through anything with her.

The first thing Brett saw was a sewn-on nametag that said "Carl." It was splotched with a dark color she knew was blood. Wordlessly, she lifted the overalls and put them to the side. Next in the bag was a complete set of clothes, including shoes, socks, pants, shirt and underwear. What was left of these was almost saturated with the same dark color. In some areas, they appeared to be crunchy with the long dried blood. Madeline covered her mouth with her hand as Brett carefully unloaded these.

Brett peered into the bag. "Bingo," she whispered.

As Allie and Madeline watched, Brett lifted a long butcher's knife from the bag. The blade was nearly rusted through, but there were still some traces of the dried blood left on it. Allie grabbed a long Tupperware container from a cupboard and Brett placed the knife inside. As Allie sealed the lid, Brett again reached into the bag.

This time she pulled out an old gun. Gingerly, she popped the barrel out and checked the bullets.

"There's one missing," she said.

Allie handed her a large plastic bag and she placed the gun in it. She pulled out a chair and sat down, staring at the pile on the table.

"I need a drink," Allie said, going into the living room. Madeline leaned against a counter staring blankly at the pile on the table.

Brett heard Allie pouring drinks for them all, then press the "Play" button on the answering machine. There were two hang-ups. Allie came back with three glasses of scotch.

As she sipped her scotch, Brett mumbled, "We were only out there a half-hour. Who could've called twice?" She felt numb. They had found what they were looking for, but she didn't know what to do with it.

Madeline looked at the pile. "I wonder how long fingerprints last for?"

"Not twenty-nine years," Allie said without hesitation. "The enzymes, amino acids and fats necessary for chemical testing would've deteriorated, and the oils and foreign substances would've been destroyed, especially in such an unprotected environment."

Madeline looked at Allie curiously. "Then why were you so careful?"

"Just in case we can find something useful, like identifying Liza's blood, or if there's hair or such."

"Yes, only Liza's blood should be in there, but maybe we'll luck out and get some real proof, like hair or tissue samples, to prove that this was Carl's uniform," Brett said, wondering why she didn't feel as if the storm inside her were over, and whether or not it would ever end.

The phone rang again. She reached over and grabbed it, irritated at the intrusion.

"Hello?" she said into the receiver.

"I understand you're very interested in Liza Swanson," the man's voice began. Brett didn't recognize it.

"Maybe I am," Brett replied, suspicious.

"Well, I may be able to help assuage your curiosity."

"Who are you?"

"Let's say I'm a friend of a friend — I know you've been asking around."

"What's your name?"

"I'd prefer to remain anonymous — for personal reasons. Can we meet somewhere?"

"Is there an all-night restaurant in this town?" Brett said. Who was this man? What did he know?

"I can't exactly remain anonymous in a restaurant full of people now, can I?"

"Where would you like to meet?"

"How about the Wright Park at midnight? Nobody should be around at that time."

"And how do I know you're not just a waste of my time?" Brett asked, worried about anyone this anonymous. The storm clouds in her mind's eye grew, with lightning scattering across the sky and thunder rumbling in the distance.

"You'll find out when you meet me. Oh, and bring your friend along." With that, he hung up.

CHAPTER SIXTEEN

"Maybe we should call the police," Madeline suggested as she paced the living room.

"No, I don't want to scare him away," Brett stated firmly.

"And you have no idea who he was?" Allie asked, frowning in concentration.

"*Nada*. But I don't think he knows which of us he was talking to."

"How do you figure that?" Madeline asked.

"He said to bring my friend. If he had known, he probably would've said 'Allie.'"

"But he might just be a homophobe," Allie remarked.

"He didn't say it with a sneer . . ." Brett replied, looking at her watch. "We've got about two hours to get ready."

"Get ready?" Madeline asked.

"I said I didn't want any police, I didn't say I trusted him."

"We don't know if he's a good guy or a bad guy," Allie explained. "And I think we should be prepared."

"And I have this bad feeling about meeting guys in parks at midnight." Brett remembered the last time she did that and it almost got her killed. "Now, if you'll excuse me a moment, there's something in the attic I want," she finished as she went upstairs.

In the attic, she switched on the light and approached the far wall, which was covered with boxes. She had to move quite a few before she found the one she wanted. It was marked "F-PT," meaning "Frankie — Paradise Theater." When they had first received Frankie's shipment, she wasn't sure why he had included these things. Now she was grateful he had. She carried the box down to the living room. She knew what she was looking for but hadn't used it in a few years and didn't want to have to keep returning to the attic for missing parts.

Madeline watched closely as Brett dug through the box, which was filled with various electronic items and other things she knew Madeline couldn't identify. She probably would've been excited, Brett thought, had she been able to recognize the lock picks and tools for breaking and entering and other destructions, but she couldn't.

When Brett pulled out what she wanted, Allie nodded in recognition. "Good idea."

Brett pulled off her shirt and Allie began her part of the job. Brett explained to Madeline, "I'm going to be wired, so we can get a recording of this." The last time she had used this particular device she was meeting with some rather unpleasant suppliers. She had had Frankie listening so he could come in and give her a helping hand if things got nasty, which they had.

"Will I be able to listen in?" Madeline asked, grinning with excitement.

"Not from this distance," Brett replied.

"But," Allie said as she taped the wires to Brett's chest, "she could sit just outside the park, so if there's trouble she can go get help."

"We could switch cars," Madeline suggested, seeing Brett's expression. "That way, I could just use your cellular phone."

Brett shook her head. "Too dangerous."

"Oh, and what you're doing isn't?"

"But —" Brett began, but Allie stared her down. She suddenly realized she couldn't say they were trained professionals, because then she'd have to explain more than she wanted to about their pasts and experiences. Already, Madeline was looking with much more interest at their equipment and actions than she was comfortable with. She gave a sigh and a shrug. "Okay, fine. We'll switch cars — but you have to follow directions precisely."

Madeline swiftly agreed.

They only had about half an hour left before they had to leave, so Brett and Allie went upstairs to finish their preparations. Brett quickly put on her shoulder holster, checked her .357 and loaded it. She slipped a very sharp knife in its own sheath on one calf, and a Beretta on the other.

Allie stood looking at the guns she had pulled out and placed on the bureau. "The big one or the little one?" she asked.

"That's easy — put the forty-four on your shoulder, and the three-fifty-seven in your pants."

Allie did so, and Brett donned her old black biker leather, while Allie wore a brown bomber jacket. When they were finished, Brett looked at Allie.

"Be careful," she said, taking Allie in her arms and holding her.

"You too," Allie said, as a tear crept to her eye at the thought of losing Brett again.

Brett pulled a little away from Allie, and held her by her arms. "You know," she whispered, her eyes moist. "The last time I met someone in a park at midnight, I got shot at, nearly raped, and all but totaled a car." As Allie stared at her wide-eyed, Brett broke into a grin. "That was the night I met you. Pretty damned good night if you ask me."

"Just think of the damage we can do now that we're a team."

Brett grinned her reply.

"So what happened to the guy you met in the park?" Allie asked as they headed downstairs.

"Frankie and I put them in intensive care for a while," Brett replied, remembering the sounds of Leo and Johnny's ribs cracking under the pressure of Frankie's weight. "They're probably retired or dead by now."

"Should I ask what you two did upstairs?" Madeline asked when they entered the living room.

Brett looked at her innocently. "No."

Madeline gave her a glare. "Someday, Brett—"

Brett raised a finger toward her. "Don't go there, Madeline . . ."

"I don't know why you keep thinking we're hiding something," Allie teased, trying to lighten the tension.

"Probably," Madeline responded, "because those jackets aren't bulky from insulation, but from what you've got on underneath them."

When they left their house in Madeline's light blue Honda, Allie watched behind them to make sure Madeline was okay in the black Ford Explorer.

Brett nervously flipped on the radio and began singing along with "I've Never Met a Girl Like You." She thought about the truth in that when she glanced over at Allie. Here she was with her woman, both reasonably armed, driving to meet some questionable fellow in a park at midnight. Were there any other beautiful women in this country who would join her on such an errand?

"Whatcha thinkin'?" Allie asked, noticing her glance.

"What would be on the soundtrack for the movie of our lives?"

"Yours would need something like 'Maniac,'" Allie replied. "We're going off to meet who knows what in an abandoned park at midnight and all you can think about is soundtracks?"

Brett shrugged and turned off the radio as they neared the park, which was only a few blocks from their home. She noticed that Madeline had shut off her lights and was parked on Downey just in front of the Church of St. Mary, according to their plan. Brett continued into the park's little dirt lot, where they left the car and headed out into the park.

Brett and Allie headed toward the center of the small park with only a small beam of light to guide their way. The moon was out, giving some light to the park. They could make out the two gazebos off in the distance and the children's play area that the citizens of Alma had constructed themselves out of high quality wood, instead of one of those cheap, obnoxious plastic ones.

Brett turned to Allie. "I wonder if this nitwit is even gonna show up."

Allie looked at her watch. "It's ten after now, I say we give him till half past."

As Brett nodded her agreement, she heard a sound behind her. Two men stepped into view from their hiding places within the play area.

"I told you they'd come," she heard the mystery caller say. She slowly lifted the light to his face. It was Charles Galliano the second, whom she recognized from the photos at Elise's, and he was standing next to Carl Swanson, a.k.a. Paul Misner. She never would've imagined that voice belonged to Jack.

Carl held a sawed-off shotgun pointed at them and Jack had his own gun pointed in the same direction. The storm in Brett's head let loose.

"Okay, you dykes, bring your hands up real slow." Carl approached them. Brett could still identify the boom in his voice, even though he was trying to be quiet. Even though he was in his sixties, he was still formidable. Both she and Allie did as they were told, even as Brett cursed herself for not paying closer attention.

"Writers my ass," Carl said as he studied them.

"Stupid bitches," Jack said. "Do you really think Elise would be so stupid as to bite the hand that feeds her?"

"What?" Allie asked. Brett wasn't sure if the tremble in Allie's voice was real or not.

"She told me all about your little visit and everything she told you. That you claimed to be writers, that she just needed to tell somebody — under the guise of anonymity and all, that is. I guess what she had done sunk in through her inebriated little mind."

Brett knew the two men were afraid she could prove they killed Liza, but why didn't Jack or Carl just come by himself? Why both of them? Except . . . "You both killed her and," she looked at Jack, "your father didn't leave you in charge of the family business because you're gay, so your brother Vinnie is the boss now."

Jack looked at her for a moment before he spoke. "Yeah. And he wouldn't be happy to know this entire problem had resurfaced. Even Elise knew she might lose everything if Vinnie got pissed enough."

"It was quite clever of you," Allie said to Carl, "to throw everyone off your tail by implicating Jen." Brett knew Allie was buying time.

This statement infuriated Carl. "She deserved to die! Recruiting the youth into her perverted lifestyle! My daughter was pure before all that. And then Jennifer soiled her with her own impurity."

199

"Carl, let's just take care of this mess," Jack said, "before Vinnie or Dad catch wind of it. They wouldn't be happy to discover that I've screwed up again."

"Yeah, the fag son screws up again, eh?" Brett asked.

Jack's eyes flared. "That mess with Liza. My father told me I was lucky she had a twin, so I could still clear things up."

But Carl was on a roll and raring to go. "They need to be taught a lesson. Taught what they've been missing while lost in their perversity. Their perversity is destroying the very fabric from which this country was created!" He turned to Jack as his fervor increased; his face was red, as if he were on the verge of a heart attack. Brett wondered if he believed this stuff, or just needed to give himself a reason to do what he wanted to do. "The public parks aren't safe anymore because of those like them, on any day of the week you can find them fornicating in the bushes — fornicating on the Lord's Day even!"

"Oh, shut up," Jack said. "Teach them anything you want to, but shove all this religious shit."

Carl gave Brett and Allie an evil grin as he sized them up. Still holding the shotgun, he began to unzip his pants. Expressionless, Jack watched him. Brett wondered why Madeline hadn't brought backups in yet.

Madeline sat cursing at the phone. It wasn't working. All she could get was static. She started the engine and raced toward the police station, praying she wasn't too late.

* * * * *

Officer John Smith didn't like his job. He liked being a cop, but he wanted to be a cop in a big city where there was real excitement. He had thought that being in the military police would open doors for him, but the only door it opened was to join the department in his home town of Alma. He longed to move on to a position in Lansing, Detroit or at least somewhere in the metro area.

But all he did these days was spend several hours a night watching for the occasional drunk driver or speeder on the streets of Alma. Most of the latter he let off because it was a small town where he knew everybody. And then, joy of joys, he also got to wander through the shrubbery at the parks, looking for kids who were drinking, smoking pot or screwing. Of course, finding the latter wasn't half bad, because, although he hated to admit it, he rather liked finding naked women in the middle of sex.

He had stopped to take a piss just behind one of the gazebos and was quickly finished zipping up when he heard voices from across the park. He moved quickly and silently, hoping to surprise them, but as he made his way around to the other side of the gazebo, just before he went into the open, he saw the moon glint off of the guns in the two men's hands.

He carefully pulled his own gun, not wanting to make any noise to draw attention to himself. Headlines of his heroism flashed through his mind. But then he heard one of the women say, "You both killed her," and John figured he should listen a bit more before he took action.

He looked longingly at the radio at his side, wishing he could noiselessly call for backup.

He recognized some of the names they mentioned from the tragic story of the Swansons'. Although he was born shortly after Liza died, he knew the names because he had often heard the story of the old haunted house.

He suddenly realized that the women in the clearing were the ones who had recently bought the old Swanson place.

Carl was moving toward Brett with his gun at his side while Jack covered him. Carl was pulling his already hard dick out of his pants when she heard a yell from the gazebo.

"Stop!"

"Who's there?" Jack yelled, whipping about to trace across the park with his gun.

Brett saw her chance. She slammed her knee into Carl's groin, then kicked the gun out of his hand with her other foot. Allie did a rolling dive to the ground in the opposite direction.

"Fucker!" Jack yelled as he fired into the distance. Brett flew to the ground, pulling her own gun.

She heard a scream as she crouched and found herself looking directly down the barrel of Jack's gun.

Before she had a chance to think or feel, there was a loud blast. She closed her eyes in a blink, sure her life was over.

She opened her eyes and saw Jack fall to the

ground. She twisted around to aim at Carl and heard another blast as something hit her leg.

Carl was recovering from the recoil of his gun when Allie blew his head off.

EPILOGUE
November 13, 1996

Brett rolled over in bed and looked at the clock. Ten minutes to midnight. Her birthday.

The anniversary of Liza's death.

She got up and quietly limped over to the window. No mysterious figures lurking by the garage. She was almost disappointed.

Carefully balancing herself to protect her injured leg, she worked her way downstairs. There weren't any dead bodies or ghosts waiting in the living room. She sat down on the couch and turned on the late show.

Her attorney was working on getting Jen out of prison. It would take a couple of weeks, maybe even a month or so, but she should be home for Christmas. Martha McDonald had been ecstatic over it all — had sent Brett flowers when she was in the hospital getting the bullet taken out of her leg, offered to do anything she could for her and Allie — but Allie told her the only thing they wanted was a family photo once Jen came home.

Jack, on the other hand, wasn't so happy. John Smith, the cop, had caught enough of their conversation to help Jen and hurt Jack. At first Brett was worried she was gonna have more mobsters pissed at her, but as it turned out, his brother Vinnie, who now ran things, and his father Charles both wiped their hands clean of him. They weren't about to come to bat or take a fall for him, not after he had disappointed them his entire life. Turned out that he had blown the chances they had given him in the family business, so they had given up and just granted him a very generous monthly stipend.

Now Elise wouldn't have that to rely on, but she'd probably get quite a bit from the divorce, plus her mother was going to sell her Colorado house and move in with her now that her father was dead. Brett hadn't really been surprised when Margaret not only did not cry at Carl's funeral, but had almost seemed happy about it. She was a free woman now, for the first time since she had been very young.

Brett looked out the window. Snow danced through

the air. The first snow of the year. Halloween was just past and now Thanksgiving, Christmas and a new year were on their way. She loved the feeling in the air, the expectation you could almost taste, at this time of the year.

You never knew quite what lay just around the corner.

She was suddenly overwrought with doubts and anxieties. What would she do now? What did tomorrow hold? She had been so immersed in this *investigation* that now she had an empty feeling, a feeling that she had lost something very important.

Twenty-nine years ago at this time Liza was still alive. Maybe she had stood looking out this very window and wondering what the future held. She would've been dreaming of running off with Jen, maybe even taking Elise with them.

Liza's future had held only death. Death and, ultimately, Brett and Allie. It was strange trying to imagine herself as someone's future. She knew what happened to everyone else involved in the situation, but not Liza. She wondered if Liza was now free to go on to whatever it was she was supposed to?

Wearing her pajama bottoms and T-shirt, Brett went over to the door, pulled on a pair of loafers and went outside. She stood on the front lawn and looked at the house. It looked like any other house.

No, it looked like their home.

"Brett." Her name was carried like a whisper across the wind. She turned to look, but only the leaves rustled in response.

Suddenly, a snowball hit her back, she whipped around and Storm's laughter carried across the wind.

Just turning the corner, running away from her, was Storm followed by Liza.

They were safe and going to where they should go.

As would she. She went back inside and curled up next to Allie.

A few of the publications of
THE NAIAD PRESS, INC.
P.O. Box 10543   Tallahassee, Florida 32302
Phone (850) 539-5965
Toll-Free Order Number: 1-800-533-1973
Web Site: WWW.NAIADPRESS.COM
Mail orders welcome. Please include 15% postage.
Write or call for our free catalog which also features an
incredible selection of lesbian videos.

MAKING UP FOR LOST TIME by Karin Kallmaker. 240 pp.
Nobody does it better . . .   ISBN 1-56280-196-1 $11.95

GOLD FEVER by Lyn Denison. 224 pp. By author of *Dream*
Lover.   ISBN 1-56280-201-1   11.95

WHEN THE DEAD SPEAK by Therese Szymanski. 224 pp. 2nd
Brett Higgins mystery.   ISBN 1-56280-198-8   11.95

FOURTH DOWN by Kate Calloway. 240 pp. 4th Cassidy James
mystery.   ISBN 1-56280-205-4   11.95

A MOMENT'S INDISCRETION by Peggy J. Herring. 176 pp.
There's a fine line between love and lust . . .   ISBN 1-56280-194-5   11.95

CITY LIGHTS/COUNTRY CANDLES by Penny Hayes. 208 pp.
About the women she has known . . .   ISBN 1-56280-195-3   11.95

POSSESSIONS by Kaye Davis. 240 pp. 2nd Maris Middleton
mystery.   ISBN 1-56280-192-9   11.95

A QUESTION OF LOVE by Saxon Bennett. 208 pp. Every
woman is granted one great love.   ISBN 1-56280-205-4   11.95

RHYTHM TIDE by Frankie J. Jones. 160 pp. . . . to desire
passionately and be passionately desired.   ISBN 1-56280-189-9   11.95

PENN VALLEY PHOENIX by Janet McClellan. 208 pp. 2nd
Tru North Mystery.   ISBN 1-56280-200-3   11.95

BY RESERVATION ONLY by Jackie Calhoun. 240 pp. A
chance for true happiness.   ISBN 1-56280-191-0   11.95

OLD BLACK MAGIC by Jaye Maiman. 272 pp. 9th Robin
Miller mystery.   ISBN 1-56280-175-9   11.95

LEGACY OF LOVE by Marianne K. Martin. 240 pp. Women
will do anything for her . . .   ISBN 1-56280-184-8   11.95

LETTING GO by Ann O'Leary. 160 pp. Laura, at 39, in love
with 23-year-old Kate.   ISBN 1-56280-183-X   11.95

LADY BE GOOD edited by Barbara Grier and Christine Cassidy.
288 pp. Erotic stories by Naiad Press authors. ISBN 1-56280-180-5   14.95

CHAIN LETTER by Claire McNab. 288 pp. 9th Carol Ashton
mystery.   ISBN 1-56280-181-3   11.95

NIGHT VISION by Laura Adams. 256 pp. Erotic fantasy romance
by "famous" author.   ISBN 1-56280-182-1   11.95

SEA TO SHINING SEA by Lisa Shapiro. 256 pp. Unable to resist
the raging passion . . .   ISBN 1-56280-177-5   11.95

THIRD DEGREE by Kate Calloway. 224 pp. 3rd Cassidy James
mystery.   ISBN 1-56280-185-6   11.95

WHEN THE DANCING STOPS by Therese Szymanski. 272 pp.
1st Brett Higgins mystery.   ISBN 1-56280-186-4   11.95

PHASES OF THE MOON by Julia Watts. 192 pp. . . . . hungry
for everything life has to offer.   ISBN 1-56280-176-7   11.95

BABY IT'S COLD by Jaye Maiman. 256 pp. 5th Robin Miller
mystery.   ISBN 1-56280-156-2   10.95

CLASS REUNION by Linda Hill. 176 pp. The girl from her past . . .
                                        ISBN 1-56280-178-3   11.95

DREAM LOVER by Lyn Denison. 224 pp. A soft, sensuous,
romantic fantasy.   ISBN 1-56280-173-1   11.95

FORTY LOVE by Diana Simmonds. 288 pp. Joyous, heart-
warming romance.   ISBN 1-56280-171-6   11.95

IN THE MOOD by Robbi Sommers. 160 pp. The queen of
erotic tension!   ISBN 1-56280-172-4   11.95

SWIMMING CAT COVE by Lauren Douglas. 192 pp. 2nd
Allison O'Neil Mystery.   ISBN 1-56280-168-6   11.95

THE LOVING LESBIAN by Claire McNab and Sharon Gedan.
240 pp. Explore the experiences that make lesbian love unique.
                                        ISBN 1-56280-169-4   14.95

COURTED by Celia Cohen. 160 pp. Sparkling romantic
encounter.   ISBN 1-56280-166-X   11.95

SEASONS OF THE HEART by Jackie Calhoun. 240 pp. Romance
through the years.   ISBN 1-56280-167-8   11.95

K. C. BOMBER by Janet McClellan. 208 pp. 1st Tru North
mystery.   ISBN 1-56280-157-0   11.95

LAST RITES by Tracey Richardson. 192 pp. 1st Stevie Houston
mystery.   ISBN 1-56280-164-3   11.95

EMBRACE IN MOTION by Karin Kallmaker. 256 pp. A whirlwind
love affair.   ISBN 1-56280-165-1   11.95

HOT CHECK by Peggy J. Herring. 192 pp. Will workaholic Alice
fall for guitarist Ricky?   ISBN 1-56280-163-5   11.95

OLD TIES by Saxon Bennett. 176 pp. Can Cleo surrender to a
passionate new love?   ISBN 1-56280-159-7   11.95

LOVE ON THE LINE by Laura DeHart Young. 176 pp. Will Stef
win Kay's heart?   ISBN 1-56280-162-7   11.95

DEVIL'S LEG CROSSING by Kaye Davis. 192 pp. 1st Maris
Middleton mystery.   ISBN 1-56280-158-9   11.95

COSTA BRAVA by Marta Balletbo Coll. 144 pp. Read the book,
see the movie!   ISBN 1-56280-153-8   11.95

MEETING MAGDALENE & OTHER STORIES by
Marilyn Freeman. 144 pp. Read the book, see the movie!
                                        ISBN 1-56280-170-8   11.95

SECOND FIDDLE by Kate Calloway. 208 pp. P.I. Cassidy James'
second case.   ISBN 1-56280-169-6   11.95

LAUREL by Isabel Miller. 128 pp. By the author of the beloved
Patience and Sarah.   ISBN 1-56280-146-5   10.95

LOVE OR MONEY by Jackie Calhoun. 240 pp. The romance of
real life.   ISBN 1-56280-147-3   10.95

SMOKE AND MIRRORS by Pat Welch. 224 pp. 5th Helen Black
Mystery.   ISBN 1-56280-143-0   10.95

DANCING IN THE DARK edited by Barbara Grier & Christine
Cassidy. 272 pp. Erotic love stories by Naiad Press authors.
                                        ISBN 1-56280-144-9   14.95

TIME AND TIME AGAIN by Catherine Ennis. 176 pp. Passionate
love affair.   ISBN 1-56280-145-7   10.95

PAXTON COURT by Diane Salvatore. 256 pp. Erotic and wickedly
funny contemporary tale about the business of learning to live
together.   ISBN 1-56280-114-7   10.95

INNER CIRCLE by Claire McNab. 208 pp. 8th Carol Ashton
Mystery.   ISBN 1-56280-135-X   11.95

LESBIAN SEX: AN ORAL HISTORY by Susan Johnson.
240 pp. Need we say more?   ISBN 1-56280-142-2   14.95

WILD THINGS by Karin Kallmaker. 240 pp. By the undisputed
mistress of lesbian romance.   ISBN 1-56280-139-2   11.95

THE GIRL NEXT DOOR by Mindy Kaplan. 208 pp. Just what
you'd expect.   ISBN 1-56280-140-6   11.95

NOW AND THEN by Penny Hayes. 240 pp. Romance on the
westward journey.   ISBN 1-56280-121-X   11.95

HEART ON FIRE by Diana Simmonds. 176 pp. The romantic and
erotic rival of *Curious Wine.*   ISBN 1-56280-152-X   11.95

DEATH AT LAVENDER BAY by Lauren Wright Douglas. 208 pp.
1st Allison O'Neil Mystery.   ISBN 1-56280-085-X   11.95

FAIR PLAY by Rose Beecham. 256 pp. An Amanda Valentine
Mystery.   ISBN 1-56280-081-7   10.95

PAYBACK by Celia Cohen. 176 pp. A gripping thriller of romance,
revenge and betrayal.   ISBN 1-56280-084-1   10.95

THE BEACH AFFAIR by Barbara Johnson. 224 pp. Sizzling
summer romance/mystery/intrigue.   ISBN 1-56280-090-6   10.95

GETTING THERE by Robbi Sommers. 192 pp. Nobody does it
like Robbi!   ISBN 1-56280-099-X   10.95

FINAL CUT by Lisa Haddock. 208 pp. 2nd Carmen Ramirez
Mystery.   ISBN 1-56280-088-4   10.95

FLASHPOINT by Katherine V. Forrest. 256 pp. A Lesbian
blockbuster!   ISBN 1-56280-079-5   10.95

CLAIRE OF THE MOON by Nicole Conn. Audio Book —Read
by Marianne Hyatt.   ISBN 1-56280-113-9   16.95

FOR LOVE AND FOR LIFE: INTIMATE PORTRAITS OF
LESBIAN COUPLES by Susan Johnson. 224 pp.
                                                ISBN 1-56280-091-4   14.95

DEVOTION by Mindy Kaplan. 192 pp. See the movie — read
the book!   ISBN 1-56280-093-0   10.95

SOMEONE TO WATCH by Jaye Maiman. 272 pp. 4th Robin
Miller Mystery.   ISBN 1-56280-095-7   10.95

GREENER THAN GRASS by Jennifer Fulton. 208 pp. A young
woman — a stranger in her bed.   ISBN 1-56280-092-2   10.95

TRAVELS WITH DIANA HUNTER by Regine Sands. Erotic
lesbian romp. Audio Book (2 cassettes)   ISBN 1-56280-107-4   16.95

CABIN FEVER by Carol Schmidt. 256 pp. Sizzling suspense
and passion.   ISBN 1-56280-089-1   10.95

THERE WILL BE NO GOODBYES by Laura DeHart Young. 192
pp. Romantic love, strength, and friendship.   ISBN 1-56280-103-1   10.95

FAULTLINE by Sheila Ortiz Taylor. 144 pp. Joyous comic
lesbian novel.   ISBN 1-56280-108-2   9.95

OPEN HOUSE by Pat Welch. 176 pp. 4th Helen Black Mystery.
                                                ISBN 1-56280-102-3   10.95

ONCE MORE WITH FEELING by Peggy J. Herring. 240 pp.
Lighthearted, loving romantic adventure.   ISBN 1-56280-089-2   11.95

FOREVER by Evelyn Kennedy. 224 pp. Passionate romance — love
overcoming all obstacles.   ISBN 1-56280-094-9   10.95

WHISPERS by Kris Bruyer. 176 pp. Romantic ghost story.
                                                ISBN 1-56280-082-5   10.95

NIGHT SONGS by Penny Mickelbury. 224 pp. 2nd Gianna
Maglione Mystery.   ISBN 1-56280-097-3   10.95

THE ROMANTIC NAIAD edited by Katherine V. Forrest &
Barbara Grier. 336 pp. Love stories by Naiad Press authors.
ISBN 1-56280-054-X 14.95

UNDER MY SKIN by Jaye Maiman. 336 pp. 3rd Robin Miller
Mystery. ISBN 1-56280-049-3. 11.95

CAR POOL by Karin Kallmaker. 272pp. Lesbians on wheels
and then some! ISBN 1-56280-048-5 10.95

NOT TELLING MOTHER: STORIES FROM A LIFE by Diane
Salvatore. 176 pp. Her 3rd novel. ISBN 1-56280-044-2 9.95

GOBLIN MARKET by Lauren Wright Douglas. 240pp. 5th Caitlin
Reece Mystery. ISBN 1-56280-047-7 10.95

FRIENDS AND LOVERS by Jackie Calhoun. 224 pp. Mid-
western Lesbian lives and loves. ISBN 1-56280-041-8 11.95

BEHIND CLOSED DOORS by Robbi Sommers. 192 pp. Hot,
erotic short stories. ISBN 1-56280-039-6 11.95

CLAIRE OF THE MOON by Nicole Conn. 192 pp. See the
movie — read the book! ISBN 1-56280-038-8 11.95

SILENT HEART by Claire McNab. 192 pp. Exotic Lesbian
romance. ISBN 1-56280-036-1 11.95

THE SPY IN QUESTION by Amanda Kyle Williams. 256 pp.
A Madison McGuire Mystery. ISBN 1-56280-037-X 9.95

SAVING GRACE by Jennifer Fulton. 240 pp. Adventure and
romantic entanglement. ISBN 1-56280-051-5 10.95

CURIOUS WINE by Katherine V. Forrest. 176 pp. Tenth Anniver-
sary Edition. The most popular contemporary Lesbian love story.
ISBN 1-56280-053-1 11.95
Audio Book (2 cassettes) ISBN 1-56280-105-8 16.95

CHAUTAUQUA by Catherine Ennis. 192 pp. Exciting, romantic
adventure. ISBN 1-56280-032-9 9.95

A PROPER BURIAL by Pat Welch. 192 pp. 3rd Helen Black
Mystery. ISBN 1-56280-033-7 9.95

SILVERLAKE HEAT: A Novel of Suspense by Carol Schmidt.
240 pp. Rhonda is as hot as Laney's dreams. ISBN 1-56280-031-0 9.95

LOVE, ZENA BETH by Diane Salvatore. 224 pp. The most talked
about lesbian novel of the nineties! ISBN 1-56280-030-2 10.95

A DOORYARD FULL OF FLOWERS by Isabel Miller. 160 pp.
Stories incl. 2 sequels to *Patience and Sarah.* ISBN 1-56280-029-9 9.95

MURDER BY TRADITION by Katherine V. Forrest. 288 pp. 4th
Kate Delafield Mystery. ISBN 1-56280-002-7 11.95

THE EROTIC NAIAD edited by Katherine V. Forrest & Barbara
Grier. 224 pp. Love stories by Naiad Press authors.
ISBN 1-56280-026-4 14.95

DEAD CERTAIN by Claire McNab. 224 pp. 5th Carol Ashton
Mystery. ISBN 1-56280-027-2   9.95

CRAZY FOR LOVING by Jaye Maiman. 320 pp. 2nd Robin Miller
Mystery. ISBN 1-56280-025-6   10.95

UNCERTAIN COMPANIONS by Robbi Sommers. 204 pp.
Steamy, erotic novel. ISBN 1-56280-017-5   11.95

A TIGER'S HEART by Lauren W. Douglas. 240 pp. 4th Caitlin
Reece Mystery. ISBN 1-56280-018-3   9.95

PAPERBACK ROMANCE by Karin Kallmaker. 256 pp. A
delicious romance. ISBN 1-56280-019-1   10.95

THE LAVENDER HOUSE MURDER by Nikki Baker. 224 pp.
2nd Virginia Kelly Mystery. ISBN 1-56280-012-4   9.95

PASSION BAY by Jennifer Fulton. 224 pp. Passionate romance,
virgin beaches, tropical skies. ISBN 1-56280-028-0   10.95

STICKS AND STONES by Jackie Calhoun. 208 pp. Contemporary
lesbian lives and loves. ISBN 1-56280-020-5   9.95
Audio Book (2 cassettes) ISBN 1-56280-106-6   16.95

UNDER THE SOUTHERN CROSS by Claire McNab. 192 pp.
Romantic nights Down Under. ISBN 1-56280-011-6   11.95

GRASSY FLATS by Penny Hayes. 256 pp. Lesbian romance in
the '30s. ISBN 1-56280-010-8   9.95

THE END OF APRIL by Penny Sumner. 240 pp. 1st Victoria
Cross Mystery. ISBN 1-56280-007-8   8.95

KISS AND TELL by Robbi Sommers. 192 pp. Scorching stories
by the author of *Pleasures*. ISBN 1-56280-005-1   11.95

STILL WATERS by Pat Welch. 208 pp. 2nd Helen Black Mystery.
ISBN 0-941483-97-5   9.95

TO LOVE AGAIN by Evelyn Kennedy. 208 pp. Wildly romantic
love story. ISBN 0-941483-85-1   11.95

IN THE GAME by Nikki Baker. 192 pp. 1st Virginia Kelly
Mystery. ISBN 1-56280-004-3   9.95

STRANDED by Camarin Grae. 320 pp. Entertaining, riveting
adventure. ISBN 0-941483-99-1   9.95

THE DAUGHTERS OF ARTEMIS by Lauren Wright Douglas.
240 pp. 3rd Caitlin Reece Mystery. ISBN 0-941483-95-9   9.95

CLEARWATER by Catherine Ennis. 176 pp. Romantic secrets
of a small Louisiana town. ISBN 0-941483-65-7   8.95

THE HALLELUJAH MURDERS by Dorothy Tell. 176 pp. 2nd
Poppy Dillworth Mystery. ISBN 0-941483-88-6   8.95

SECOND CHANCE by Jackie Calhoun. 256 pp. Contemporary
Lesbian lives and loves. ISBN 0-941483-93-2   9.95

BENEDICTION by Diane Salvatore. 272 pp. Striking, contemporary romantic novel.   ISBN 0-941483-90-8   11.95

TOUCHWOOD by Karin Kallmaker. 240 pp. Loving, May/
December romance.   ISBN 0-941483-76-2   11.95

COP OUT by Claire McNab. 208 pp. 4th Carol Ashton Mystery.
                                                           ISBN 0-941483-84-3   10.95

THE BEVERLY MALIBU by Katherine V. Forrest. 288 pp. 3rd
Kate Delafield Mystery.   ISBN 0-941483-48-7   11.95

THE PROVIDENCE FILE by Amanda Kyle Williams. 256 pp.
A Madison McGuire Mystery.   ISBN 0-941483-92-4   8.95

I LEFT MY HEART by Jaye Maiman. 320 pp. 1st Robin Miller
Mystery.   ISBN 0-941483-72-X   11.95

THE PRICE OF SALT by Patricia Highsmith (writing as Claire
Morgan). 288 pp. Classic lesbian novel, first issued in 1952 . . .
acknowledged by its author under her own, very famous, name.
                                                           ISBN 1-56280-003-5   10.95

SIDE BY SIDE by Isabel Miller. 256 pp. From beloved author of
Patience and Sarah.   ISBN 0-941483-77-0   10.95

STAYING POWER: LONG TERM LESBIAN COUPLES by
Susan E. Johnson. 352 pp. Joys of coupledom. ISBN 0-941-483-75-4   14.95

SLICK by Camarin Grae. 304 pp. Exotic, erotic adventure.
                                                           ISBN 0-941483-74-6   9.95

NINTH LIFE by Lauren Wright Douglas. 256 pp. 2nd Caitlin
Reece Mystery.   ISBN 0-941483-50-9   9.95

PLAYERS by Robbi Sommers. 192 pp. Sizzling, erotic novel.
                                                           ISBN 0-941483-73-8   9.95

MURDER AT RED ROOK RANCH by Dorothy Tell. 224 pp.
1st Poppy Dillworth Mystery.   ISBN 0-941483-80-0   8.95

A ROOM FULL OF WOMEN by Elisabeth Nonas. 256 pp.
Contemporary Lesbian lives.   ISBN 0-941483-69-X   9.95

THEME FOR DIVERSE INSTRUMENTS by Jane Rule. 208 pp.
Powerful romantic lesbian stories.   ISBN 0-941483-63-0   8.95

CLUB 12 by Amanda Kyle Williams. 288 pp. Espionage thriller
featuring a lesbian agent!   ISBN 0-941483-64-9   9.95

These are just a few of the many Naiad Press titles — we are the oldest and largest lesbian/feminist publishing company in the world. We also offer an enormous selection of lesbian video products. Please request a complete catalog. We offer personal service; we encourage and welcome direct mail orders from individuals who have limited access to bookstores carrying our publications.